NOBODY

KNOWS

ALSO BY MARY JANE CLARK

Do You Want to Know a Secret?

Do You Promise Not to Tell?

Let Me Whisper in Your Ear

Close to You

NOBODY

—— KNOWS ——

MARY JANE CLARK

Bookspan Large Print Edition

ST. MARTIN'S PRESS ❧ NEW YORK

This Large Print Edition, prepared especially for Bookspan, Inc., contains the complete unabridged text of the original Publisher's Edition.

ISBN 0-7394-2899-3

**This Large Print Book carries the
Seal of Approval of N.A.V.H.**

Again, for Elizabeth and David

ACKNOWLEDGMENTS

At the start, there was only a mental image of a little boy with a metal detector finding something in the soft Florida sand. What it was he found, I did not know, nor did I have any idea where the discovery would lead. Getting from that initial idea to the book you now hold in your hands required help. To those who came through with essential assistance when I needed it, my sincere thanks.

Father Paul Holmes, independent editor, did not look askance at me when I told him about my vague vision. Paul encouraged me and brainstormed with me through a tough autumn when real world events seemed far stranger and more terrifying than anything this writer could dream up. His support was unflagging.

Jim Murphy, executive producer of the *CBS*

Evening News with Dan Rather, generously shared his experience and insights on what the ethical and legal ramifications are for running with a controversial story ahead of the competition.

CBS news correspondent Bobbi Harley came to my rescue again, this time providing lots of colorful descriptions of working in Miami and covering hurricanes.

Those Federal Bureau of Investigation sources keep wanting to remain nameless, but another special agent took time to explain to me the workings of the FBI's Fugitives List.

As deadline approached, Mary Catherine Ryan came through with immediate research assistance, as did Elizabeth Higgins Clark, my daughter.

Laura Dail makes the "business" of writing so much more fun than it otherwise would be. I couldn't ask for a more nurturing, energetic, capable agent and, now, good friend.

And while we're on the subject of business and friendship, Colleen Kenny came into my life years ago as my children's baby-sitter, grew to be a friend, and has developed into a first-class Web master, showering her conscientious attention on www.maryjaneclark.com.

The contribution of Jennifer Enderlin is formidable. I know I am fortunate to have such a talented and creative editor. Jen was able to pinpoint areas where the story needed more fleshing out, and her expert suggestions definitely make *Nobody Knows* a more compelling read. I can't thank her enough for the care she has taken with this project, beginning with conceptualizing the cover, which art director Anne Twomey executed to perfection. As always, it makes me feel better to know that Sally Richardson, Matthew Shear, and John Murphy are on my side at St. Martin's Press.

Finally, if Jane and Bennett Willis had not introduced me to the beauty that is Sarasota so many breathtaking sunsets ago, I would not have had firsthand experience of this luscious locale, the place where my precocious child finds something in the sand. To Aunt Jane and Uncle Bennett and my family and dear friends, "nobody knows" where I would be without you.

NOBODY

KNOWS

PROLOGUE

Tuesday, February 19

From the time she'd been old enough to understand what it was, she was afraid of it. All women were. It was brutal, invasive, destructive, and too horrible to wrap your mind around.

Rape was all these things, but it was not a federal crime.

Something didn't feel right here. KEY News Justice Correspondent Cassie Sheridan waited for the press conference to begin, already knowing from her FBI sources that a rapist was being added to the Fugitives List.

Strange, thought Cassie as she watched Pamela Lynch, clad in a severe gray business suit, take the platform at the front of the crowded pressroom at the J. Edgar Hoover Building. While the director was known to announce additions to the infamous Ten Most Wanted List, the Fugitives List didn't warrant the same attention. Why was the FBI's first female director facing the press herself on this one?

Pamela Lynch ran her fingers through her cropped gray hair and cleared her throat as the din of the press people subsided.

"Good afternoon, everyone," she began, looking directly out into the audience. "The FBI realizes the value of public assistance in tracking down fugitives. Since the establishment of the Federal Bureau of Investigation's Ten Most Wanted List over fifty years ago, we are approaching five hundred fugitives listed. Almost a quarter of those individuals have subsequently been apprehended as a direct result of citizen cooperation."

Cassie scribbled on her notepad as the director continued. "The criteria for selection are fairly straightforward. First, the individual must have a lengthy record of committing serious crimes and/or be considered a particularly dangerous menace to society due to current criminal charges. Second, the FBI must believe that the nationwide publicity can be of assistance in apprehending the fugitive."

Lynch stopped to reach beneath the podium for the glass of water waiting there. As the director lifted the glass to her mouth, Cassie, sitting in the front row, noticed that Lynch's hand was quivering. *She can't possibly be anxious about this, can she?* Pamela Lynch was known to have nerves of steel. Cassie had watched her many times as she faced tough questioning about terrorism and unflinchingly defended attacks on FBI conduct. Why would Pamela Lynch be unnerved by a fairly routine news conference on domestic wrongdoing?

"We have no picture of the individual that we are looking for. When we get one, if he isn't apprehended first, I can assure you he will be elevated to the Ten Most Wanted List. As you know, no individual is placed on the Ten Most Wanted List without a picture."

I didn't know that, thought Cassie.

"Today we ask for national cooperation to help the FBI track down a new, as yet un-named, member on the FBI's Fugitives List. We are calling him Emmett Doe. The composite drawings you see here are based on the descriptions given by some of the victims of his crimes."

Flashbulbs popped and cameras whirred as Lynch gestured toward two blown-up images arrayed on easels. One was an artist's rendition of a man's face, the other was a drawing of the face of a frowning clown. The reporters murmured among themselves as they studied the grotesque, exaggerated features of the second drawing.

"Emmett Doe is being sought for car theft and rape in Louisiana and Florida. These crimes occurred within the past six months. Doe is considered armed and extremely dangerous. We are asking anyone who has any information about this individual to, please, contact your local FBI office or, if outside the country, the nearest U.S. embassy or consulate."

Hands shot up in the audience.

"Yes," said Lynch, pointing to the CBS correspondent sitting beside Cassie.

"Is there a reward being posted?"

The director nodded. "The FBI is offering a reward of up to fifty thousand dollars for information leading directly to the arrest of this individual."

"You have the eye color listed as blue *and* brown. What does that mean?" asked another reporter.

"Two of the victims say their attacker had blue eyes. The other victim reported brown. We're not sure of the man's true eye color."

Cassie raised her reporter's notepad into the air. Pamela Lynch looked directly into her eyes.

"What details can you give us about the rapes?"

Lynch fumbled with her papers on the podium. "This individual raped a young woman from the Miami area last November. He struck again in New Orleans earlier this month. As you know, rape is a crime, but it is not a federal offense. So, technically, the rapes are not what earned Doe a place on this list. The fact is that Doe is a menace to society and we think the public can help us catch him."

Cassie had a follow-up. It seemed like the obvious question. "Will you explain to us the derivation of these artist sketches?"

The director cleared her throat. "Ah, yes," she answered. "The victims describe a man of medium height and build, who wore a grease-painted mask in the image you see here." Lynch pointed to the clown poster. "FBI artists then tried to estimate what the man looked like beneath the makeup. This is what they've come up with." She gestured toward the other easel.

In the audience, the CBS correspondent leaned over and whispered to Cassie. "Pretty nondescript-looking face."

Cassie agreed. There was nothing distinctive about the face that glowered from the poster board.

"Can you describe for us his M.O.?"

The director took another drink of water before answering. "All three women were attacked where they lived, at night, after they had gone to sleep. The attacker tied them up and gagged them with their own undergarments. Then he"—Lynch stopped to swallow—"then he raped them at knifepoint. Afterward, he took their car keys. The abandoned vehicles were later found at city airports."

A new question: "How common is it for a rapist to disguise himself?"

"It's not common. Our Behavioral Science Unit at Quantico has found that the majority of serial rapists don't dress in any special way. We're trying to figure out what the significance of making himself up as a clown might have for this vicious individual."

It was after five o'clock when New York finally gave script approval, leaving Washington less than an hour and a half to get Cassie's piece edited. Cassie recorded her track and left her producer and videotape editor in the editing booth to finish putting the story together while she went back to her office and made another call to the press information office at the FBI.

"You're on his list, Ms. Sheridan," said the secretary, weariness in her voice.

"This is the third time I've called. Please, have him get back to me. I need to speak to him before we air."

"I understand, Ms. Sheridan. I'll be sure to give him your message."

At six o'clock, Cassie sat in the makeup chair, being touched up for her live studio appearance scheduled at the end of her story. The stylist was spraying Cassie's black hair when Yelena Gregory's large frame appeared in the doorway.

"I found someone else to have lunch with," the news president said, smiling.

"I'm so sorry, Yelena," she apologized, totally bummed out that the press conference had forced her to cancel their third meeting to discuss the possibility of Cassie's being elevated to the network's premier newsmagazine show. "I hope we can reschedule something."

Yelena walked into the room and over to Cassie's chair. "I have to fly back to New York right after the broadcast." At the look of disappointment on Cassie's face, Yelena reached out and patted the correspondent's wrist. "Don't worry, Cassie. Everything is a go. Business Affairs will be contacting your agent. We want you on *Hourglass*."

Cassie strode to the editing room and viewed the completed piece. It was well constructed, covering all the apparent bases. But over fifteen years of journalistic experience told Cassie that there was something else to this story. She had learned to trust her gut.

The story was scheduled for the second

news block, after the first commercial break. At six-fifteen, as Eliza Blake mounted the *Evening Headlines* anchor platform in New York, Cassie tried the FBI again. She didn't call the bureau's press office this time but instead called her friend Special Agent Will Clayton.

"I'm on deadline, Will, and the press office isn't returning my calls. I need to know, what was with Pamela Lynch this afternoon?"

"What do you mean?"

"Come on, Will. I have to go on air. The director doesn't normally make these announcements. And she was shaking like a leaf."

"She's personally invested in this one, Cassie."

"Meaning?"

There was silence on the line.

"Will? Come on. What gives?"

"I guess it will come out sooner or later. I'm surprised none of the other networks picked up on this." Clayton hesitated.

"What? What will come out?" Cassie urged.

"You didn't hear it from me."

"Fine. I didn't hear it from you. What is it?"

* * *

"How old was she?"

"Twenty-one. She was a senior at Loyola University in New Orleans."

"I don't see how we can't report it, Cassie," said Executive Producer Range Bullock from the Fishbowl in New York. "One of the highest-ranking law enforcement officers in the country is using her power to take care of personal business. That's *huge* news under any circumstances. Would that kind of action be taken for any regular American family?"

"Would any regular American family have their daughter identified as a rape victim?" Cassie countered, squirming at the thought of using Maggie Lynch's name on the air.

Range popped an antacid tablet in his mouth. "This isn't a regular case. Even if this guy belongs on the Fugitives List, the FBI director's daughter is the victim, and that's a major story."

"I don't feel good about this, Range."

"None of us do, Cassie. But it's news, and it will get viewers. The other nets will eventually pick up on it and report it anyway."

In Washington, Cassie hung up the phone. *Viewers and ratings,* she thought. So often, it came down to that. The battle for higher ratings and the advertising dollars that followed. This was February, a sweeps period, and *Evening Headlines* was more focused than ever on pulling in the audience.

She hurried into the studio and slid into her seat. Catching her breath and clipping the small microphone to her jacket lapel, she watched Eliza Blake on the monitor. In her mind, Cassie composed what she would say when the camera switched to her. After the last pre-narrated video of Cassie's report finished rolling, her hazel eyes stared directly into the dark lens and she began.

"It's unusual for the FBI director to announce personally an addition to the Fugitives List, but this was not a usual situation for Pamela Lynch. KEY News has learned that Lynch's only daughter, Maggie, was one of the victims raped by the man with the painted face of a clown."

Listening to Jim's even breathing from the other side of the bed, Cassie stared into the darkness, unable to sleep. After a day like the one she'd just had, she was pumped. She had scored an exclusive with the Pamela and Maggie Lynch information. Range had called from New York after the broadcast, heavy with praise.

More important, she was going to New York to star on *Hourglass.* Though Jim and Hannah had been less than enthusiastic when she told them her news tonight, she convinced herself they would come around. The much larger salary she'd be pulling down would soften the blow. Jim wouldn't even have to work if he didn't want to. He could spend more time on his writing. And Hannah would make new friends.

Opportunities like this were rare. Though it meant uprooting her family, Cassie hungered for the new job, one of the most coveted positions in network news.

The move to New York might be good for the marriage, she rationalized. A fresh start in a new place. It might force them to depend on one another again.

Like the old days.

Cassie closed her eyes, willing sleep to come.

The screech of the telephone pierced the darkened bedroom. She reached over to grab the phone, hoping that Jim wouldn't wake.

"Hello?" she whispered.

"Cassie? It's Steve Wagner on the assignment desk."

"Yes?"

"I'm sorry to wake you, Cassie, but you should know. Maggie Lynch jumped out the window of her mother's apartment at the Watergate tonight."

Thursday, August 15

The boat rocked, soothing her, as she held her manicured hand up to catch the soft light from the moon. She admired the brand-new ring that sparkled from her finger. The ruby in its golden setting matched the shade of her nail polish.

Merilee had recognized the name on the jeweler's box. The priciest store in town. He must have paid a pretty penny for this ring. It was clear he was smitten with her, exactly as she intended him to be.

On the deck, she waited alone for him and dreamed, looking out at the lights twinkling from the shoreline, humming the tune she hoped would make her rich. She had big plans. A hit song, a piece of the action of Web of Desire Productions, and one way or another, a well-to-do husband were all in Merilee's design for her future.

Whatever was he doing down there for so long?

She went below to find him, quietly sliding open the louvered door.

"What are you doing, sugar?" she purred before she had time to take in the horror of his reflection in the small mirror that hung over the sink. White powder covered his face, garish blue makeup encircled his brown eyes.

Caught, he spun to face her as she backed away in revulsion. His teeth looked yellow and nasty against the red of the painted mouth as he tried to persuade her that nothing was wrong.

But this was wrong. All wrong.

What kind of sick freak was he? The monster who stood before her certainly wasn't the man she thought she knew. This man clearly had a side she had never seen before. A twisted, demented side. She had to get away.

Merilee turned her back on him and scrambled up the ladder to the deck, sensing that he followed close behind. She considered jumping out into the dark waters of the Gulf, but the shore was far away and she didn't know how to swim.

Trapped.

With no other choice, Merilee turned on the deck to confront the grotesque visage. "Get away from me, you sick freak."

As he edged closer, his eyes flashed with rage at her stinging words.

Merilee's face contorted in pain as his powerful fist smashed against her smooth cheek, the force of the blow knocking her against the railing of the rocking boat. She shook her head, desperately trying to clear it, as the clown reached down and grabbed her.

MONDAY

August 19

CHAPTER
1

Vincent blinked his brown eyes, groggily adjusting to the early morning light that slipped through the space between the window frame and the frayed vinyl shade. The first thing he heard was the comforting drone of the air conditioner. The second thing he heard was the familiar sound of his brother's cough.

Kicking off the cotton blanket, Vincent sat up, threw his legs over the side of the twin mattress, and stared at his younger brother lying in the companion bed crammed into the small room. Unmindful of his latest coughing episode, five-year-old Mark still slept. Vincent supposed the kid had to sleep through it if he was to get any rest at all. Mark had been hacking through the night, every night, for as long as Vincent could remember.

Many nights the eleven-year-old would listen in the dark to the coughing coming from the next bed. He was afraid that his brother was getting worse. He resented that Mom focused so much of her attention on Mark. He was angry that he had to help with his little brother when every other kid his age seemed to be out playing without a care in the world. He was relieved that he didn't have the same condition that afflicted his brother. And then, ultimately, he felt guilty. Why did Mark have cystic fibrosis? Why had Vincent been spared?

The doctor at the clinic had tried to explain it. Some people unknowingly carried the defective CF gene. Both mother and father had to have the gene and pass it on to their baby. Mark had gotten the sickly combination. Vincent had not. It was just the luck of the draw.

Some luck, thought Vincent as he quietly pulled on his shorts. His brother had an incurable disease, his mother was worried all the time, and he hadn't seen his father since three Christmases ago.

Careful not to make any noise, Vincent stepped gingerly over Mark's inhaler on the bedroom floor. He couldn't wait to get to the beach. He hoped he hadn't missed anything good by not going late yesterday afternoon after the swimmers and sunbathers left. That was the time to go, at the end of the day, the time with the best chance of finding the good stuff. But Mom had to go into work early to cover for one of the other waitresses who'd called in sick and Vincent had to stay with Mark and give him the treatment with the pounder.

Vincent hated the pounder, the electric chest clapper that helped dislodge the mucus that built up in Mark's lungs. But the pounder was a lot better than the old-fashioned way Mom used to do it, clapping and pounding on Mark's chest with her fists. Three times a day for twenty to thirty minutes each time. Little as he was, Mark never complained. In fact, he said it didn't hurt. But Vincent cringed to watch it.

Mom tried to make the time go faster by singing songs with Mark. For Vincent, television was the preferred diversion during the pounding treatments, as much to keep *his* mind off what they were doing as to distract his brother.

The door to his mother's bedroom was open, and Vincent stepped though the doorway. A ceiling fan whirred over Mom's bed, moving around the sticky air. There was only one air conditioner in the small, rented cottage and the boys had it in their room. Mark's condition demanded it. Vincent supposed that was one plus. Another was the mini-trampoline that lay on the living room floor. Mom had bought that for Mark to jump up and down on to supplement his chest physical therapy, which gave Vincent a chance to play around on it, too.

His mother stirred in her bed and, in her fitful sleep, muttered something that Vincent could not understand. He walked over to the bed. Her blond hair was tangled on the pillow, and there were dark smudges under her eyes left by the mascara she hadn't bothered to wash off when she got home last night. Jumbled together on the floor at the foot of the bed were white sneakers, denim shorts, and a black T-shirt with the bulldog mascot of The Salty Dog stenciled across the front.

Vincent tiptoed to the dresser and counted the carefully stacked bills that lay on top of the chipped paint. Forty-eight dollars. Hardly worth the night's work. But that was August in Florida. During "the season," when Siesta Key was crowded with all the northerners who came down to escape the miserable winters in their home states, a dinner-shift waitress at The Salty Dog could bring home two hundred dollars for serving frosty beers, clam chowder, shrimp poppers, fish-and-chips, and battered, deep-fried hot dogs to the steady stream of customers who came to the informal open-air restaurant.

Mom worked the dinner shift so she could be home with Mark during the day while Vincent was at school. But Mark, already reciting the alphabet and beginning to sound out words, was about to start full days himself. Vincent hoped Mom would keep her promise to work more lunches and, when the snowbirds returned to Siesta Key in November, go back to cleaning houses and condos for extra money so she could stay home with them at night. He didn't want to admit it to anyone, but it was scary sometimes being home taking care of Mark. Scary and time-consuming and distracting. Vincent's grades had fallen over the past year, and the teacher had told Mom that, with the material getting harder, he needed more help with his homework.

Vincent was tempted to wake his mother and tell her where he was going, let her know that he was forced to get up so early to get to the beach and see if he could make up for missing yesterday. Instead, he took a pencil and scribbled a note on the back of the envelope that had the bill in it from the telephone company. One of the many bills lying unopened on the cracked linoleum counter. As he headed out, Vincent stopped to strap on his rubber-soled sandals and grabbed the metal detector propped up next to the front door.

Though the air inside his house was warm, the whirring ceiling fans made it bearable. The air that greeted Vincent outside was oppressive, even at this early hour. The heat and humidity enveloped him as he walked down the front steps and onto the road heading toward the beach. He had gone just two blocks when he felt the first trickle of perspiration drip from his temple. By the time he got to the next corner, the back of his neck was wet.

The streets were quiet. Most mornings there would have been a few joggers out, but today it seemed that not even the most devoted wanted to brave the heat. Vincent recognized the haunting cry of a mourning dove, though he couldn't tell where the eerie coo was coming from. A gecko scampered across the sidewalk in front of him, eager, Vincent supposed, to get off the baking macadam and onto the cooler grass.

Vincent noticed the scattered vacancy signs in front of the rental condominiums and bungalows. August might be a busy time of year at northern beaches but not at Siesta Key. Compared with the winter and spring, summer made a relative ghost town of Sarasota's barrier island.

For Vincent, August meant that vacation time was over and school would soon be starting again. Next week, to be exact. He felt a lump in his throat as he thought about it. A sixth-grader now, he would be going to the middle school, at the lowest rung of the ladder, with all the seventh- and eighth-graders above him. Vincent was keenly aware that he was small for his age, but at least last year he had been on top of the elementary school heap. Now he was going to be at the bottom. He had heard that middle school was brutal. He didn't want to go.

He crossed over Beach Road and passed a trash can full of discarded Budweiser cartons and bottles before he stepped onto the white sand. The sand of Siesta Beach was famous, and Vincent was proud of the fact. One year, Vincent knew, Siesta Key had been chosen Best Overall in the International Sand Contest, competing with exotic places like Barbados, Antigua, and the Grand Bahamas for the title. Siesta Key's sugary sand, composed of billions and billions of tiny crystals, was judged to be the finest and whitest in the competition. Now Vincent scuffed through the prized soft powder and switched on the metal detector.

He had to give it to his mom, he thought, as he swept the detector over the sand. She tried to do the best she could with the money she made. She was always going to garage sales and picking up things he could use. A bike, a skateboard, a tennis racket, a snorkel mask and fins. This metal detector was, with the exception of his bicycle, the sweetest thing she had ever found. She had bought it and put it away and given it to him on his birthday in June, apologizing that it wasn't brand new. Vincent couldn't have cared less. All summer long he had been sweeping the beach. Every day was a treasure hunt.

Mostly the giant wand found lost change. Quarters, dimes, and nickels and pennies that Vincent rinsed off in the water of the Gulf of Mexico and stuffed into his pockets until he went into the village and spent them on chocolate ice cream cones at Big Olaf's or threw them into the empty coffee can on top of the dresser he shared with his brother. The instant money was good, but jewelry was even better. It made Vincent feel like a pirate, finding buried treasure.

So far his summer booty had included a gold cross and chain, a Timex watch, a silver bracelet, and lots of single earrings. One earring had a diamond in it. Gideon had taken him to a jewelry store on the Tamiami Trail and the man there paid fifty bucks for it!

This morning, oblivious to prehistoric-looking pelicans skimming the green water, the gulls pecking in the sand for food, and the cloud-dotted blue sky stretching as far as the eye could see out over the Gulf, Vincent swept the metal detector back and forth over the beach, dreaming of making another great find. The machine sounded off, and

Vincent dug beneath the fine grains to un-cover a metal comb. He tossed it aside. Next he found a quarter. And then another. He slipped them into his pocket.

He made his way up the beach toward the Old Pier, Gideon's favorite place to fish for pompano and permit. But the old fisherman wasn't there. Vincent cut in across the beach toward the worn, concrete seawall. He'd found good stuff at the foot of the seawall before, stuff that had been swept in by the tide.

A mound of green and black seaweed lay clumped at the bottom of the wall. Vincent passed the metal detector over it, and the in-dicator went off. Not relishing the idea of picking up the slimy sea grass, he cast around for something to do it for him. The neck of that discarded beer bottle would do the trick.

Vincent squatted down, inserted the brown glass beneath the seaweed, and pulled back. At first he thought what he saw had to be a fake. He bent down closer. No, it was real, all right. The boy took a deep breath and gagged.

Oh, sick! This was nasty.

Nestled in the prizewinning soft, white

sand, a gold ring with glittering red stones gleamed in the morning sun. The ring constricted the finger of a swollen human hand.

CHAPTER
2

The sunrise. Thank God for the sunrise.

At least for a few minutes as Cassie ran to the end of the dock that zigzagged out into Biscayne Bay, the magnificence of the sun rising over the blue-green water into Florida's spectacular sky made everything else seem utterly unimportant. For those few moments every morning, Cassie had the relief of being able to fill her mind with the sunrise and push away the memories of what had happened. Her life was a wreck, and Cassie couldn't see that she'd ever be able to straighten things out.

A stranger passing Cassie on her morning run through the already hot and humid Miami Shores streets wouldn't know the pain she was in by looking at her. Five months into her assignment as KEY News Miami Bureau correspondent, Cassie was in far better physical shape than she had ever been in Washington.

The daily three-mile runs that she took to maintain her sanity and clear her mind had firmed her up and trimmed her down. Though she rarely got to the beach, she had a glowing tan, the result of all the outside work she was doing in her new assignment. In her old life, Cassie never had a tan. As justice correspondent, she'd spent most of her days in climate-controlled offices. She'd gone from reporting from the sheltered FBI headquarters or the Supreme Court on stories with national implications to standing sunburned and thigh-high in muck in El Salvador mud slides or picking through the debris left in Louisiana trailer parks ravaged by tornadoes. Such was the scope of the Miami Bureau. Cassie could be called on to cover anything that happened in the southeastern quadrant of the United States as well as Central and South America.

It would have been a big help if she had spoken Spanish. But she didn't. Her high school Spanish had long since left her, and she hadn't given it much mind. In Washington everyone spoke English, of course, and Washington was where she belonged. Washington or New York, that is.

She had loved her job as KEY News justice correspondent, but she had been ready for a professional change. Covering the Supreme Court, the Justice Department, and the FBI was challenging and stimulating, especially in the months after the terrorist attacks. Cassie's pieces had been on *Evening Headlines* almost every night, reporting developments in the investigation, describing the new world of anthrax and wiretaps and Level One security alerts, Most Wanted lists of international terrorists and multimillion-dollar rewards for their capture. With the exception of the anchorwoman, Eliza Blake, Cassie had had more airtime since the attacks than any other female correspondent at KEY News. It would have been satisfying to leave the Washington Bureau on such a high note.

Cassie was aware, too, that her clock was ticking. Now that she was thirty-nine years old, the once open vistas of broadcast journalism had begun to feel a bit more limited. The network chiefs could say what they wanted, but they were still more likely to put older men than older women on the prime-time news shows.

Yes, it had seemed just the time to make the switch and move to New York.

But then the Maggie Lynch story had changed everything, making all Cassie's big career plans seem so inconsequential. A young girl was dead, and Cassie had played a part in that. As a mother herself, she could understand Pamela Lynch's agony and rage and her need for justice. The rapist was still out there somewhere, hidden and anonymous, but Cassie was front and center, a target for vengeance. A deserving target.

Cassie winced as she turned her back on the hopeful sun and started across the dock to the shore. She had to get home, if you could call the apartment that. She needed to shower, dress, and force herself to go to a job that was a constant reminder of her failure.

Waiting for her at the end of the dock was the sunburned man, dressed in his stained red Bermuda shorts and loose-fitting, red-and-black Hawaiian shirt. He wore the same clothes, black sneakers, and dirty socks that he'd worn yesterday and the day before and the day before that. Glazed blue eyes shone from his ruddy, weather-beaten face. Steel gray hair was pulled back in a matted pony-tail, pieces of dead grass sticking from it. His lips were cracked and discolored.

God knew where the man slept at night, thought Cassie, but he made it a point to be waiting at the dock for her every morning since she had given him that first five-dollar bill. Cassie stopped and pulled a folded bill from beneath her wristband.

"Make sure you get something good to eat with that today, okay?" she urged as she handed him the money. The man nodded.

When their ritual had started, shortly after she had moved to Miami, Cassie had tried to find out more about the man. What was his name? Where did he live? How had he ended up where he was? But her questions had been met with silence and, eventually, she didn't ask anymore. She couldn't force the man to talk to her, but it gave her some peace of mind to give him the money. She just had to hope that he really did buy food and didn't blow it on booze.

Didn't the poor creature have anyone who cared about him? It was so sad and so scary. *There, but for the grace of God, go I.*

Cassie shivered as she jogged away. *Life sure turns on a dime. I could end up where that man is. Anyone could.*

All those years she had worked hard to accomplish what she had professionally, so many times at the expense of her personal life. Now her profession had hung Cassie out to dry, and her husband and daughter weren't there for her either. She couldn't blame Jim or Hannah, really. They had formed their own special bond during Hannah's formative years. Jim had simply spent more time with their daughter. Jim Sheridan, high school English teacher, with his predictable hours and long summer vacations, had done more of the day-to-day raising of their child, helping Hannah with her homework, coaching her softball team, taking her to dance lessons and doctors' appointments. The beeper that Cassie always wore had sounded too many times, calling Mommy to work, calling the wife away from her husband.

Cassie rationalized that it was her work that had allowed Hannah to have all the advantages. While Jim made a respectable salary, it was Cassie who brought home the real bacon, earning five times what her husband did. That income made their four-bedroom, three-bathroom brick colonial in Alexandria possible. That income paid for her Saab convertible and Jim's Volvo station wagon. That income had paid for Hannah's summer camp when she was younger and for the shopping sprees at Abercrombie & Fitch now. That income was paying for all that was going on in the home that Cassie wasn't a part of anymore.

Because, now, Jim wanted a divorce, thirteen-year-old Hannah wanted to stay with her father, and KEY News had transferred Cassie out of her beloved Washington Bureau to Miami, where she was marking time while she and KEY News were being sued for the wrongful death of Maggie Lynch, the daughter of the first female director of the Federal Bureau of Investigation. Yep, life could turn on a dime.

CHAPTER
3

The freshly shaven face peered back at him in the makeup mirror. It was important to start with a clean, dry face.

He dipped his finger into the white grease-based makeup and began to smooth it around his eyes and mouth, careful to use only a little bit. Too much would look heavy. Once the round shapes were applied, he used his fingertips to pat, helping the makeup get into the pores and smoothing out the streaks. Next he took a Q-tip and swirled it in his mouth to moisten it. The saliva-sharpened tip outlined the white painted area, making it more distinct.

Picking up an old tube sock filled with the baby powder he had taken from Maggie Lynch's bathroom, he shook it over the area he had made up and applied the sock to his face to press in the precious dust. He sat back and contemplated his reflection as he waited a minute for the powder to sit. Then he took a brush and flicked off the excess. Next, he applied the flesh-colored makeup to the rest of his face, except the area around his nose where the red would go. He repeated the routine of patting with his fingertips and powdering, followed by drawing black lines around his eyes.

He picked up a theatrical makeup pencil and colored in a red, down-turned mouth and filled in a red circle over the tip of his nose. He didn't have time this morning to bother with the prosthetic nose. He picked up the spray bottle from the dressing table and misted his face. Some blue around the eyes to make the clown's face look scarier and a mascara wand to his eyelashes and the work was done.

He turned his head from side to side and admired himself in the mirror. What would his mother say if she could see him now? Something mean and screeching, to be sure. *The harridan.*

He ached to get out there again and find someone, see the expression on a young woman's face as she looked up at him. But for now he had to gratify himself with the makeup alone. He knew the FBI was still looking for him, and it worried him. How could he have known that the pretty coed he followed home from the Mardi Gras parade was the daughter of the FBI's director? How could he have known that he would end up all over the national news?

"I won't harm you if you cooperate."

She had listened, her eyes bright. She didn't know that he didn't really plan on using the knife. But the knife worked well. Women were terrified at the prospect of disfigurement.

"Tell me that you love me."

She had put up no struggle. As she lay there, his pleasure increased. Maybe she did love him, maybe she enjoyed it. Just like the girl in Miami and the last one in Louisville.

He didn't want to be caught and was fighting hard to hold back. He was using all his willpower to keep himself from finding another woman.

Merilee and what happened on the boat didn't count. That was different.

CHAPTER
4

Breathing heavily and dripping with perspiration, two blocks from her high-rise, Cassie slowed down to walk the rest of the way. Aware of the checks she had to send to Jim twice each month and the fact that the checks from KEY might stop coming after the Pamela Lynch lawsuit was over, Cassie had chosen a less expensive apartment than she would have at another time. She'd found a sparsely furnished one-bedroom with rent much less than it would have been if it were on the west side of Biscayne Boulevard, where most of Miami Shores was—the side with the manicured lawns, palm trees, and Spanish-style houses. Cassie's condo tower community was on the east side of the boulevard, where the neighborhood was not so highbrow. She passed several one-room shacks as she turned into her building's driveway.

Inside, she switched on the coffeemaker, flipped on the television, unwrapped *The Miami Herald,* and spread it out on the kitchen counter. She stood in her running shorts, perusing the newspaper from front to back, periodically looking up to aim the remote control at the TV and click around to the various morning news shows. Cassie paused as the radar map of Florida shone bright green from the screen.

"Here in the Miami area, we'll have another hot one. Temperatures should reach the high nineties with eighty percent humidity."

A different weather map popped up. On this one, Florida appeared smaller, making room for the Atlantic Ocean on the east coast and the Gulf of Mexico on the west. The weather person pointed to the southern Gulf. "There's a tropical storm here, folks, and it seems to be gathering steam. This one has the potential of developing into a hurricane. We'll be keeping an eye on it and will keep you posted."

Cassie sighed as her mind speedily calculated what this could mean to her. If a hurricane developed, she would have to cover it in all its unpredictable, wind-whipping, flooding glory. A hurricane would mean property damage and possible loss of human life, and Cassie would have to report on it. If the hurricane were powerful enough and horrible enough, Cassie would be up to her neck with it, and with the havoc it left in its wake, through the coming weekend, perhaps into next week.

She had planned to fly up to Washington to see Hannah this weekend, since Hannah wouldn't come down to see her. The last thing she needed right now was her teenage daughter experiencing yet another example of Cassie's work getting in the way of their lives.

She glanced at her watch and considered calling her daughter but thought better of it. With school starting soon, these were the last mornings Hannah would be able to sleep late. She'd wait and call her from the office.

Yes, they could go shopping together for school clothes this weekend, Cassie thought as she swallowed the last gulp of coffee. A normal mother-daughter thing to do. That was what they needed. Some uninterrupted time together, just the two of them, doing ordinary things.

And, though she hated to admit it, even to herself, she wanted to see Jim too. She missed him. Missed the sound of his deep voice, missed the way his eyes crinkled at the corners when he laughed. She missed the all's-right-with-the-world feeling she used to have when he took her hand in his. There had been many sleepless nights over the past months, and Cassie had yearned to reach out and find him in the bed beside her, ached to feel the warmth of his strong arms wrapped around her in the dark.

The cruel things they had said to each other at the end were fading in memory, replaced with flashbacks to the happy times they'd shared. She'd first spotted him in that Advanced Shakespeare class back at Georgetown, the earnest expression on his handsome face as he listened intently to the professor expound on *Romeo and Juliet.* She'd watched as he took notes and raised his hand to enter the discussion. His comments impressed her. The next week Cassie casually took a seat near his. By the end of the spring semester, they were inseparable.

Oh, what a spring that was. Falling in love

in Washington as pink cherry blossoms popped around the tranquil Tidal Basin, as balmy breezes caressed their faces and ruffled their hair on their long walks together. The hours they'd spent talking over cups of coffee, the alleged study dates that had turned instead into make-out sessions behind the library stacks.

Cassie treasured those sweet memories, and the ones that came after. The cramped apartment with its futon and old theatrical posters dotting the walls. The fun they'd had going to tag sales and used-book shops, trying to save money. Their budget might have been tight on Jim's initial teaching salary and Cassie's paltry income from her first job as a desk assistant at *The Washington Post,* but they'd felt confident about their future. Back then, it had all stretched before them.

From the newspaper Cassie had gone on to a researching job at KEY News, which led to an associate producer's spot. The fact that she was talented and bright was complemented by the fact that she was also very pretty. Within a few years she was doing on-air pieces for the weekend news broadcasts.

The joy of finding she was pregnant was tempered by worries about what it would do to her career. Yet her heart had felt as though it would burst through her chest at the sight of Hannah's damp head in the hospital delivery room. Yes, she had been torn about going back to work after her too-short, six-week maternity leave. But Cassie could also not deny the large part of herself that was hooked on the television news business, enjoyed the office and the stimulation and camaraderie she felt there.

It had been a fine, but flawed, balancing act, juggling the demands of family and career. She should have seen it coming, should have known that something had to give. *Please, please, please,* she thought. *I've paid my dues. Paid them over and over and over again. Please, no cancellations this time. Don't let this thing turn into a hurricane.*

CHAPTER
5

A cupful of coffee from 7-Eleven in his hand, Sarasota County Sheriff's Deputy Danny Gregg let himself into the small office in the pavilion on Siesta Public Beach. The start of another hot day in what promised to be another hot week.

In his late twenties, good-looking and solidly built, the young officer was very pleased with the career path he had chosen. His job as one of the ten sheriff's deputies assigned to Siesta Key offered Gregg a somewhat flexible schedule, a variety of experiences, and for the most part, a feeling of satisfaction every day. At the end of a shift, he always had an answer when Colleen asked him what had happened at work. A shoplifter caught in Siesta Village, a traffic accident at the approach to the causeway, a child temporarily lost on the beach.

Danny liked that he had four modes of transportation available to him to carry out his job. He had a white police truck to patrol residential neighborhoods and answer traffic calls. A bicycle to pedal through the village and make sure all was well in the blocks of colorful T-shirt stores, informal restaurants, and gift shops. A Jet Ski to get around in the water that surrounded and reached into the key. And his olive green ATV, his all-terrain vehicle with the oversize rubber tires that gripped the sand as Danny cruised the beach at will.

He had no set schedule. No one looked over his shoulder to make sure he was at a certain spot at a certain time doing a certain thing. Danny had been chosen for the Siesta Key beat because his bosses in the sheriff's department had observed the young deputy to be a self-starter, conscientious and dependable. They didn't want a guy who was lazy by nature and looking for ways to goof off.

Danny put the paper coffee cup down on the desk and adjusted the leather holster on his belt. He even liked his uniform of forest green shorts and white golf shirt with SARASOTA COUNTY SHERIFF DEPARTMENT, DEPUTY D.

GREGG, embroidered in the same dark green over the right breast. How many sworn officers of the court got to dress like they were going out to shoot eighteen holes?

He was slathering on some sunscreen over his tanned forearms when the dispatch call came in. "Proceed to Old Pier. Human hand found at the seawall."

"Say again?"

"Caller says a male youth found a severed hand."

As Danny climbed onto his ATV, his wife, safe at home with Robbie, their eight-month-old son, flashed through his mind. He'd really have something to tell her tonight.

The ATV sped up the relatively empty beach, leaving its distinctive tire print in the damp sand. Scattered early morning walkers and joggers, a few shell collectors, and lots of seabirds occupied themselves on the shoreline. But as the deputy got closer to the northern tip of the beach, he could see a cluster of people gathered at the seawall. The small crowd parted as Danny dismounted the sand cruiser.

A sandy-haired kid, whom Danny judged to be about nine or ten years old, stood proprietarily next to the clump of seaweed.

There was something familiar about the boy, but Danny couldn't quite place him.

"I found it, mister, but I put the seaweed back on top of it, so the sun wouldn't bake it," the boy said with pride, bending down to pull away the thick grass. The officer stopped him.

"That's okay, kid. I'll take over now. Okay, everybody. Stand back," Danny ordered. The onlookers inched away, wanting to stay close enough to get a good view. The deputy slipped on a rubber glove and swallowed before he lifted the greenish vegetation.

It was a hand all right. The stench was awful.

The hand had been through only the good Lord knew what. The crowd was growing now as every curious resident or vacationer who had ventured out on the beach that morning was eager to see what was going on.

Danny rose from his crouching position. "Come on, folks, move along now. Please, move along."

As far as the deputy could tell, no one moved. So much for obeying authority. He needed to get some help. This was no one-man job. He pulled out his radio and called the supervisor. "We need some detectives and somebody from the crime scene forensics unit out here."

While he waited for backup, Danny started the paperwork. He took the initial offense report form from the aluminum strongbox fastened to the back of the ATV, filling in the date and time. Then he asked the boy his name.

"Vincent. Vincent Bayler."

"How old are you, Vincent?"

"Eleven."

On the small side for eleven, the deputy thought. This kid looked like he spent a lot of time outdoors. The tips of his eyelashes were bleached white. So were the hairs on his bronzed arms and legs. Danny stared at Vincent, still not able to put his finger on where he had seen the boy before. "Address?"

"603 Calle de Peru."

Now he remembered. He had responded to a call at this kid's house last winter. This Vincent had called 911 when his little brother had some sort of coughing attack. Yeah, that was it. The little guy had cystic fibrosis.

The mother had left the older brother in charge while she was working. But, to her credit, Danny remembered, she'd come running when her son phoned her. She was the one who told Vincent to call the police while she was on her way. The deputy and the mother had arrived at the tiny bungalow at about the same time. It had been raining. He recalled the sound of the heavy tropical raindrops falling on the tin roof, persistent background noise for the younger boy's racking cough.

The call had ended with a ride to the hospital emergency room, where the sheriff's deputy had left the family of three. Danny was ashamed now that he had never followed up to see how they had made out. But, as he recalled it, that was the night before Colleen gave birth to Robbie. Yeah, he remembered clearly now. Looking at his healthy baby in the nursery bassinet and saying a silent prayer that his tiny son would never have to go through the agony that the little Bayler boy had gone through the night before.

Now, the deputy regarded Vincent's solemn face with respect and compassion.

For an eleven-year-old kid, Vincent had a

lot of responsibility. It couldn't be easy hav-ing a brother as sick as that. Plus, there didn't seem to be any father around. There was an air of sadness about the boy. Too sad and too serious for a young kid.

Deputy Gregg could not know that Vin-cent was trying with all his might to keep the solemn expression on his freckled face as he answered the officer's questions. He re-counted how he had discovered the hand and then flagged down a jogger and asked him to find a telephone and call the police. The deputy noticed that the boy told his story with his fists clenched and stuffed into the pockets of his baggy shorts. But he couldn't see that Vincent's left palm was closed around the ruby ring the boy had twisted and pried from the severed hand be-fore he called for help.

CHAPTER
6

Showered, dressed, and made up, Cassie drove her Ford Explorer through the guardhouse and clicked her battery-powered opener to raise the security gates. On the way out to Biscayne Boulevard, she stopped for gas at the Texaco station that also served as a mini–grocery store. A working girl's best friend, the convenience store had milk, juice, bread, snack food; it even stocked a decent wine selection. Cassie didn't like to recall how many times she had stopped on her way home after a long day and picked up a bottle of Kendall-Jackson Merlot knowing that it would keep her company for the rest of the evening.

As she inserted the nozzle into the gas tank, she thought with a pang about why she'd chosen this vehicle from the used-car lot. She had purchased the gold-colored

SUV when she arrived in Miami because it was relatively cheap and would have space for the gear for all the things she told herself it would be great to take up. Scuba diving, sailing, golfing, weekend trips to the Keys. Things that Cassie hoped would lure Hannah down to visit. Activities and trips that hadn't materialized. Hannah had refused to come down. Cassie hadn't had the desire to follow through on the planned activities on her own.

"I'll take a lottery ticket, Manuel," she said as she paid the cashier.

"You feel lucky, señora?" The cashier smiled as he handed her the ticket.

"Yes, Manuel, so lucky. You wouldn't believe how lucky I feel." She tried to keep the sarcasm from her voice.

At the beginning of the five-mile drive south from her condo to the office, Cassie passed a country club, a few churches, and a couple of shopping centers. Then the neighborhood took a decided turn for the worse as she drove by sleazy, no-tell motels. It wasn't that Washington didn't have any seamy neighborhoods, Cassie reflected. Far from it. But Cassie didn't have to drive through any on her way to and from work every day. Her life had changed dramatically, and she was still shell-shocked.

If she felt like a sleepwalker going through the motions of her day-to-day existence, Cassie wondered how Pamela Lynch was faring. Any FBI director was held under a magnifying glass, but for the first female director the scrutiny was ratcheted higher still. Pamela Lynch was expected to do her job each day, and though it was tragic that her daughter had killed herself, in the end no one but her family and friends really cared. The press corps wouldn't give her any passes if she fouled up. She had to perform every day, whether her heart was broken forever or not. In that way, Cassie supposed, she and the powerful woman who was suing her were a lot alike. Of the two of them, though, Cassie knew she had the better deal. She would rather be herself, tangled though her life might be, because Pamela Lynch's daughter was dead and nothing could bring her back. Cassie's Hannah was alive, and Cassie still had a chance to make things right between them.

For the rest of her life, Cassie knew she would regret Maggie Lynch's death and the part she had played in it. She could try to rationalize it with the belief she had been doing her job and the public had a right to know that the director was using the FBI to find her daughter's attacker. Yet a young woman whose promising life lay before her couldn't face a world that knew her secret. A secret that Cassie had broadcast to the entire country.

Cassie wished, oh how she wished, that she could turn back the clock.

Though she was extremely worried about the lawsuit, part of Cassie felt she deserved to be sued. If the reverse had happened, and something Pamela Lynch said or did had contributed to Hannah's death, a lawsuit would be a poor substitute for the more visceral urge to use her bare hands to take revenge on Lynch.

The voice from the Explorer's radio pulled Cassie from her reverie. "That tropical storm in the Gulf of Mexico is building quickly. They're calling it Giselle. Winds are being clocked at seventy miles per hour."

Cassie had a sinking feeling in the pit of her stomach.

CHAPTER
7

Most mornings Etta Chambers came home from her early morning search on Siesta Beach with her plastic bag filled with a nice assortment of shells. Turkey wings and whelks, conches and cockles and lion's paws. Occasionally she came across an un-broken black sand dollar or a starfish. Since they were still alive, Etta always threw those back into the ocean. But today there was very little in Etta's shell bag. Her search had been interrupted by the ruckus at the beach.

"Charles? Charles!" she called out as she came through the front door of the town house she shared with her husband of forty-seven years. "Charles, where are you?"

"I'm out here, Etta. Where I am every morning when you come home from the beach, honey."

Etta followed her husband's voice to the

screened lanai, where Charles sat with his feet up in a lounge chair reading the newspaper. "Charles, you'll never guess what happened!" she said, continuing on before he had a chance to respond. "A woman's hand was found on the beach. You know that boy we always see with the metal detector? He found a woman's hand!"

Charles closed the *Sarasota Herald-Tribune* and put it in his lap to listen to Etta's story. The boy, the seaweed, the police. Charles was impressed by Etta's description of the hand and the fact that his usually squeamish wife had gotten so close and taken in the gory details so thoroughly.

"The hand was all bloated and some of the fingertips were actually missing," said Etta, her eyes wide. "But I think there was a delicate bone structure beneath the puffiness. And I'm sure it was a woman's hand because there was bright red polish still painted on some of the fingernails. I think she was a racy kind of woman, Charles. There was a little black spiderweb painted on the pinkie nail." Though it was growing warmer by the minute on the lanai, Etta rubbed her bare arms as she finished relating what she had seen. "You don't think this kind of thing happens around here much, do you, Charles? This is the type of thing we wanted to get away from up north."

"Etta, we've been here almost a year now, and this is the most exciting thing that's happened yet."

"Exciting? How can you say it's exciting? It's horrible!"

Charles shrugged. "All right. Horrible. It's a horrible thing, Etta, but I'm sure it's not reflective of life down here. And, as a matter of fact, I wouldn't say that we retired down here to get away from this sort of thing up north. McLean, Virginia, wasn't exactly the inner city, dear. We came down here to get away from the cold and the gray winter days and because the kids had moved out so there wasn't any sense in having that big house anymore. Now we don't have to rake leaves, shovel snow, or scrape ice off the car."

Etta waved at her husband dismissively. "You know what I mean, Charles. I like to think of this as our little island paradise." She looked through the screen out to the expanse of green water that led to the Gulf. A heron swooped gracefully across the sky. "I don't want crime and ugliness to invade our world here, Charles. We've worked very hard, and now I want to sit back and enjoy life. I don't want to worry about murder and someone lopping someone else's hand off."

"Who said anything about murder?" asked Charles. "Maybe the poor soul had an accident or committed suicide."

Etta paused to consider her husband's theories, but it wasn't long before she was distracted. "What time is it?" she asked sharply.

Charles glanced at his gold watch. "Almost nine."

"Oh. I have to get into the shower," she said, forgetting the hand on the beach for the time being. Forgetting until she got up to the Ringling grounds and could tell the other volunteers who staffed the art museum, the circus museum, and Cà d'Zan, the former winter residence of John and Mable Ringling. Etta had hurried to get involved as soon as they moved down here. She worked at the gift shop or staffed the admission desk, and she was studying to become a docent. She looked forward to being able to give visitor tours and answer questions about the history of the Ringling family and about John Ringling himself, the man who had forever linked the circus with Sarasota.

"You won't forget to meet me at Dr. Lewis's office at eleven-fifteen, will you, Charles?"

"Don't worry, Etta, I'll be there."

Etta turned and went back into the town house and up the stairs as her husband rose from his lounge and walked slowly from the lanai through the living room and into the galley kitchen. He pulled a quart of orange juice from the refrigerator and poured himself a tall glass.

"Ahh," he said to no one but himself. The orange juice just plain tasted better down here. So did the fruit and the vegetables and the chicken.

Charles shook his head as he went back into the living room and switched on the TV. He couldn't believe how much time he spent thinking about the quality of his food these days. For four decades of his job as a contractor, he hadn't cared what Etta served for dinner at night—as long as it was ready when he got home. Now, not only did he care but he was doing most of the shopping and cooking.

He had to admit Etta had been making more of a life for herself here than he had. Not only did she volunteer at Ringling but she had joined a book club and a garden club. She had made friends, and Charles had the distinct feeling that she could be doing more with her new pals if she so desired. He'd heard her turn down telephoned luncheon invitations many times. When he'd asked her why she was declining, Etta had pecked him on the cheek and told him that she'd come to Florida to spend her days with him. It was her husband she wanted to be with, she said, but still, she knew they couldn't be together every minute. They would drive each other insane.

It would be healthier if he found some outside interests, too, Charles thought as he settled into the big chair across the room from the television. But what? He had never taken up golf, and truth be told, he wasn't exactly enthusiastic about learning now. Maybe fishing? He should track down that old fisherman who was always at the beach and see if he would share his knowledge.

The retiree's attention was diverted by the Suncoast News meteorologist, who was talking about the tropical storm in the Gulf of Mexico and explaining the storm grading system. "Winds up to thirty-eight miles per hour, that's a tropical depression. If winds reach thirty-nine miles per hour, that's a tropical storm. When a tropical storm reaches a constant wind speed of seventy-four miles per hour or greater—that's a hurricane.

"Stay tuned, folks, and we'll keep our audience in the Sarasota Bay area up to speed on how Giselle develops."

CHAPTER
8

Cassie drove into the parking deck underneath the fifteen-story bank building that housed what was left of the KEY News Miami Bureau and gave the garage attendant a quick *"Buenos días."* She eased the Explorer into her designated slot, next to the one marked EL JEFE, the space for the boss. But the latest round of corporate layoffs had eliminated the head count for a Miami bureau chief. Senior Producer Leroy Barry had inherited the boss spot. Leroy's parking space was empty.

The bundle of newspapers was waiting near the elevator, and Cassie picked it up. *The Miami Herald, The New York Times, USA Today,* and *The Washington Post.* It stung every morning to see the masthead of what had been her hometown paper. Cassie had to force herself to go through the *Post*'s pages, reading about people with whom she had been on a first-name basis, people who'd always returned her calls, people who didn't want to know her anymore. Once, Cassie had influence and power in the Beltway world; now she was weak. In an environment based on power and access, weakness was repulsive. Even those who sympathized with her situation were uncomfortable associating with her, and Cassie knew it.

She was a leper.

If she had paid more attention to her family and less to the job, it would be different. She would have drawn strength and emotional sustenance from a loving relationship with her husband and daughter. But she had neglected both Hannah and Jim. She hadn't meant to, but she had. Everything at KEY News had seemed so damned important. It was so easy to get sucked in. The broadcasting adrenaline was addictive and intoxicating. Now, especially without her family, withdrawal was excruciating.

Yelena Gregory had tried to make the Miami assignment sound positive when she broke the news that it was her decision, as president of the news division, that Cassie move from the Washington Bureau, but not to New York as planned. Both women, though, knew the truth.

It was fine to be stationed as Miami correspondent on the way *up* the news ladder. But Cassie most definitely was on the way down. Wanting to make a point, Pamela Lynch was suing KEY News along with Cassie for $100 million. KEY News was sticking with Cassie while the case was in the courts. But after that, Cassie suspected she'd be on her own, cut loose by the company she had worked for most of her professional life.

How quickly things change, she thought as she got off the elevator on the eleventh floor and walked along the outside terrace to the office. Six months ago she was on track for the spot on *Hourglass.* Her agent had been salivating about going into the next contract negotiations. Now he didn't return her calls.

Cassie punched in the security code at the front door, which unlocked with a buzzing sound. She entered the dark and depressing space. A large office, meant for dozens of staffers, was now used by only a handful. Because of the leaner operation across the board, the KEY corporate stock was doing well. Cassie knew this because she was suddenly paying attention. The shares she had accumulated over the years would be up for grabs in the divorce proceedings.

Her office was off to the side of the no-longer-busy central newsroom. She went in and whipped through the newspapers, listened to her voice mail, and checked her e-mail. Next she scanned her computer for the *Evening Headlines* early rundown. Cassie felt another catch in her throat as she saw that Valeria Delaney was slated to do a story from the Justice Department. Valeria was an ambitious young thing, and she was lobbying hard for the justice correspondent title officially left unfilled since Cassie's departure.

Cassie pushed the phone pad keys and

waited for further humiliation. She had to keep calling the Fishbowl, pitching story ideas, and see if they'd bite.

"Bullock," came the curt answer.

"It's Cassie Sheridan, Range." Why did she feel like a nervous kid when she got the executive producer on the line?

"Yeah, Cassie. What've you got?"

She knew Range was just going through the motions with her, though neither of them wanted to acknowledge it. Almost every story Cassie had proposed since she had been in Miami had been flatly rejected. The reasons given had varied, but she knew the bottom line: they didn't want her on the air. Not unless it was to do the miserable stories that no one at her stage of the game really wanted to do. For those awful natural disaster stories, the Fishbowl would use her.

"There's a story in the *Herald* this morning, Range, about the FBI's Organized Crime/Drug Program investigation of drug trafficking here in Miami. I thought I'd call around and see what I could come up with on it."

There was a momentary pause on the line.

"Range?"

"I think it would be best if Valeria worked on this one, Cassie. Why don't you give her a call and ask her to check things out with the FBI?"

Oh God, the morning's humiliation was now complete. She took the pen she had been holding and jammed it in her palm.

But Range wasn't finished with her yet. "Cassie, what's the deal with this tropical storm in the Gulf? From the sound of it, we better get in position over there."

She'd been avoiding it. If she didn't bring it up, maybe it would go away. Yeah, right. But she didn't want to think about the possibility of a hurricane. She wanted to see Hannah this weekend. Cassie was only thirty-nine, she reasoned with herself. Hannah was only thirteen. There was still time to make things right between them.

But in Miami, as in Washington before, work called the shots.

CHAPTER
9

The arrival of the Suncoast News Network crew added to the hubbub on Siesta Beach. Trudging through the sand and dripping with perspiration, the SNN photographer-editor Brian Mueller followed his reporter. They couldn't locate the kid who had found the hand, but they recorded an interview with a sheriff's deputy and got reaction from people on the beach.

"I think it was a shark," said one woman.

"This is a helluva way to start the day," said a man who identified himself as a vacationing New Yorker.

The guy's right, thought Brian. This was a crappy way to start what was going to be a long, long day. Once they got enough here, they'd have to hurry back to the station and put together the story for noon. Then the news director would have the bright idea that the piece should be updated for the six o'clock hour, so they'd scarf down some lunch, then go back out and try to find some new element to advance the story. Then rush back again to the station, edit and feed into the show. But that wouldn't be the end of it.

Brian had to shoot that charity event at the Ringling mansion tonight where the Boys Next Door were going to play. He had to get all those society types arriving for cocktails on the Cà d'Zan terrace. He'd be lucky if he was home by midnight.

"They aren't paying me enough," Brian muttered under his labored breath as his reporter pointed toward the sheriff's investigators walking away from the seawall, signaling that the photographer should get the shot.

Brian hoisted the camera up to his shoulder, aimed in the direction of the officers, focused, and recorded a shot that pushed in on the case an investigator carried. The hand was wrapped up in that case. Gross.

Nope, Brian thought, SNN wasn't paying him enough to do the stories he had to drag himself out on. And certainly not enough for the twelve- and thirteen-hour days he routinely put in, or for the road trips that the news director expected him to make during sweeps periods. But the job did give him re-spectability. Brian liked to tell everyone he worked in the news business, though his larger source of income came from some-where and someone else.

The flashy red sports car he drove sig-naled to his outside friends that he was do-ing quite well, but the people who worked in the newsroom with him were puzzled. Each had an idea of what the others were mak-ing, and Brian Mueller was not making enough at SNN to afford a Corvette and that prime condo he was renting right on the water. They didn't know Brian made his real money moonlighting for Webb Morelle. Webb paid big and the work was enjoyable, but editing X-rated movies didn't go over well with most folks. Pornography, exotica, adult entertainment, whatever you wanted to call it—if you mentioned that you worked on sex videos, people thought you were a pervert.

Not that a lot of those same judgmental people weren't watching the porno flicks themselves. Webb was always boasting that pornography in the United States was bigger business than pro baseball, basketball, and football put together. Lots of people were watching, but no one admitted it.

"Hey, Brian, I think that's him!" called the reporter, motioning toward a skinny kid walking from the direction of the road to the seawall accompanied by a white-haired yet robust-looking man sporting a mustache and wearing the long-sleeved shirt, pants, and brimmed hat of a fisherman. When the boy and his companion reached the wall, they stopped, and Brian recorded a long shot of the boy pointing and gesturing as he talked to the old man.

The reporter approached the boy. "Are you the one who found the hand?"

Vincent nodded.

"Mind if we ask you a few questions?"

The old guy interrupted. "Who are you and who do you work for?"

For just an instant the reporter looked crestfallen, and Brian tried not to smile. The reporter liked to think that everyone in Sarasota watched him on television and knew who he was. *Well, they don't, buddy. Get over yourself.*

"We're with SNN. I'm Tony Whitcomb. This

is for a report on the noon news today, and I'm sure it will be on again tonight."

The fisherman looked at the news pair skeptically, but the kid was champing at the bit to talk. "Come on, Gideon," said the boy. "I'll be on TV!"

"Maybe you should check with your mother first," suggested the old man.

The boy hesitated and looked up at Whitcomb for his reaction.

The reporter glanced at his watch. "We've got to get back to the station, kid, so we don't have a lot of time. How 'bout I give you my card and you call me and tell me if your mom doesn't want you to be on TV?"

Gideon shrugged, and Vincent eagerly began to tell his story for the SNN camera. The boy made no mention of the ring.

CHAPTER
10

Just as the operator called to connect the Miami Bureau to the conference call with the Fishbowl in New York, Leroy Barry dropped his knapsack on his desk, unzipped it, pulled out a can of Coke, and popped open the flip top. He put the phone on speaker, hit the mute button, and settled back in his chair, lifting his feet up onto his desk. He wasn't going to be called upon to speak, so he could relax.

The drill was the same every day. The conference call was designed to fill in the domestic news bureau personnel on what was being worked on throughout the United States and the rest of the world to air on the *KEY Evening Headlines with Eliza Blake* that night. The Los Angeles Bureau chief spoke first, listing what was going on in the western half of the country. Next came the

South and North editors, speaking from their desks in New York on what they had on the agenda based on their calls with the Miami, Chicago, and Dallas Bureaus and information gleaned from the KEY affiliated local news departments in their regions. Then the Washington senior producer chimed in with what was going on in the nation's capital. Range Bullock rounded out the call with news of foreign coverage and any *Fresher Looks* or special stories not mentioned by anyone else.

With a notepad and pen in hand, Cassie slid into the only other chair in Leroy's cluttered office as the call began. It was a busy news day. Los Angeles had sent a reporter and crew to Montana to cover forest fires raging there. In the Northeast, West Nile virus was popping up again and a heat wave was smothering the northeast corridor. Washington had at least three stories that looked like they would make air tonight. The president was returning from a NATO summit meeting, the Pentagon was releasing new successes on the terrorist target front, and the attorney general was zipping around on personal business on a chartered private jet at taxpayers' expense. Leroy thought he noticed Cassie cringe when it was announced that Valeria Delaney was covering that one.

"We have spectacular volcano eruption pictures from Mount Etna," Range declared. "Fabulous flowing lava and scorched earth. Gerald Mazza will have a package from Sicily on that."

Cassie noticed that Leroy was absent-mindedly clicking his pen. A bad sign. He was eager to have a story. Leroy was always eager to have a story. He knew that a running list was kept in New York of the number of pieces each producer and correspondent put together. He also knew that having a high count would hold him in good stead come next contract negotiation. More important, his ego demanded that his packages regularly air. In the past five months his story count had dwindled, and they both knew why. The Bowl wasn't using Cassie, and Leroy resented the hell out of the position that left him in.

He angrily stabbed the button on the phone console, ending participation in the conference call. "With a little luck, that storm

will keep building," he said. "I can't stand waiting around here. I want to cover some news."

Cassie said nothing.

Will Clayton took Cassie's call as he had
every Monday morning for the last six
months, out of a sense of gratitude and obli-
gation and perhaps to ensure that she
wouldn't go public. If the director knew that it
was he who had given Cassie the information about Maggie Lynch, he would be finished at the FBI. But, so far, Cassie had
refused to reveal the source of her information. Will wanted to make sure it stayed that
way.

"How ya doin', Cassie?"

"I'll be much better if you tell me there's
something new."

"I wish I could, Cassie. I wish I could. The
director is on the warpath about it."

"God, Will, I can't believe you guys
haven't figured this out yet."

"Give us a break, will you, Cassie? We
don't have all that much to work with. Three
cases. That's it. Maggie Lynch in February,
the one before that last November in Miami,
and the one this spring in Louisville. The guy
is really spreading things out."

Cassie thought of the details of the latest attack, in May. The same M.O. as the others. A young woman, followed home at night, waking to a knife at her neck, the grotesque clown's face breathing into hers.

"The makeup could have been purchased anywhere, and the airline rosters didn't show any name recurring on flights from those cities on those dates," Will continued, defending the bureau's investigation. "The best leads we have come from the victims' statements. The fact that the duration of each attack increased with the victim's passivity, that he promised not to hurt these women if they complied, and asked them to tell him that they loved him—all of this suggests to us that he is a compensatory rapist."

"What's that?" Cassie interrupted.

"It means he's not your everyday scare 'em, tear 'em attacker. We think this guy's core fantasy is that the victim will actually enjoy the rape and fall in love with him. Because of his inadequate personality, the rape assuages the doubts he has about himself. The big problem is that when this clown's—excuse the pun—when his need for reassurance arises again, it will be time to go out and find somebody else to make him feel better about himself."

At the end of their conversation, Cassie hung up in frustration. This rapist had to be caught, before he savaged another woman's life. And if he was found, she might, please God, be able to stop feeling so guilty.

CHAPTER
11

With Lou-Anne on her way to the hair salon and the kids escorted by the mother's helper to story hour at the library, Webb Morelle had the spacious multilevel condo to himself. He poured a third cup of coffee, lacing it with half-and-half and three sugars, cut a generous wedge of iced coffee cake, grabbed a paper towel for a napkin, and lumbered down the steps from the kitchen that led to his home screening room. Webb lowered himself onto the huge sectional sofa, clicking the remote control as he raised his pajama-clad legs onto the marble coffee table.

The opening credits popped onto the big screen encased in the custom-built wall unit. "Merilee We Roll Along," proclaimed the title. "A Web of Desire Production."

Webb loosened the sash of his silk bathrobe and settled back into the plush cushions to enjoy the show. The surround sound created an acoustic environment that made Webb feel as though he was experiencing the action on the screen. He smiled, becoming increasingly certain at each grunt and groan that *Merilee We Roll Along* was going to be another big moneymaker.

This was the second video in which Webb had cast Merilee as his star. The first, *Merilee, Merilee, Merilee, Life Is But a Dream,* had been the best-selling video Web of Desire Productions had ever had. Webb didn't kid himself that the script he had written was the secret to the movie's success. Nor was it the dry ice machine that made the misty clouds enveloping the actors as they went through their contortions, nor that shredded angel costume that Merilee wore. The secret was Merilee herself, and her cloud of dark hair and tawny velvet skin that stretched over a tight body that didn't quit. It was Merilee with her deep brown eyes and playful expression that dominated that video. The camera loved her, and she loved the camera right back.

Webb watched the giant screen now as Merilee wrapped herself around her partner in porn, Van Jensen. No doubt about it. This would be another hit, even if it turned out to be the last time Merilee starred for Web of Desire Productions.

He clicked off the video, tossed the remote on the table, and laid his head back to rest on the top of the sofa. Webb stared at the ceiling and the multicolored mural painted there. Lou-Anne had paid a pretty penny to have those entertaining scenes depicting Sarasota's circus history. Trapeze artists and elephants and ringmasters and clowns, all under the big top. The source of inspiration for some of the many video stories that had made the Morelles millionaires. Lou-Anne often used this room to entertain the ladies from her various social committees. If those women only knew what really paid for all the catered luncheons down here and the thick carpet on which they parked their Ferragamos.

He knew his wife was mortified at the thought of the socialites finding out what he did for a living. She demanded Webb's secretary answer the office telephone with the generic "Production Company." She insisted that they make contributions to many of the local charities, which were all too happy to accept his fat checks. She told anyone who asked that her husband made motivational sales videos for corporate clients. *Yeah, right,* thought Webb. *They're motivational all right. The biggest motivators of all.*

God, there was money to be made in this business! He'd bet that though he'd barely made it to graduation, he was making more now than most of his Ivy League classmates who had graduated at the top of their class and worked at the nation's most prestigious law firms and corporations. Funny how life turned out. Twenty years ago he'd taken that part-time job at the off-campus video store, and the rest was history. The English major found that he spent a good deal of time answering the questions of customers who wanted to know how to tell one adult videotape from another. The VCR was starting to find its way into more and more American homes then, and Webb was sure its popularity was driven, to some degree, by the easier and more anonymous access it offered to porn. Before home video, pornography had a much smaller audience, mainly men, who sneaked into sleazy movie houses and took care of business under their raincoats. The VCR made it easy to watch porn in the privacy of your own bedroom. At the same time, the spread of AIDS was frightening many men—and women—from sallying forth into the world for their sexual adventures. For many watching porn equaled safe sex.

Webb saw an opportunity and seized it. He was sure there would be a huge market for adult videos. Why spend his time sweating over the great American novel, unsure that he would ever find a publisher to print it or an audience to read it? That was for the guys who didn't care if they ate or not. Webb knew he wanted the good life, and the good life cost plenty. If he could write and produce his own adult movies, he'd always have an audience for his creativity, and at the same time he could make a fortune.

He'd started by conducting a verbal survey of his fraternity brothers on what they'd like to see in a porno flick. Cheerleaders and pretty coeds in short skirts and tight sweaters seemed to be the prevailing preferences. He then scribbled out a rough script about a nerdy-looking guy who went to class and fantasized about a beautiful girl who sat in front of him. Next Webb sought out a couple of kids from the wrong side of the tracks who were anxious to make some money and willing to do what the script called for, dressing the guy in a Dartmouth sweatshirt and the girl in a tight T-shirt. He shot his first movie with a camera he "borrowed" from the school audiovisual department. *Dee Dee Does Dartmouth* became a fraternity row hit.

While other classmates were doing internships at the companies and brokerage firms in which they hoped to find jobs upon graduation, Webb spent his summer before senior year writing and sending away for college sweatshirts. *Yolanda Does Yale, Happy Does Harvard,* and *Pia Does Princeton* were dubbed and distributed by winter break. America sure was the land of opportunity.

As Webb's life had progressed, so had the porn. The Ivy League series had led to *Office Girls* as he pumped his friends for their thoughts about the women they worked with in their first jobs. There was an endless pool of fantasies about secretaries and co-workers and supervisors set on the office desks and in boardrooms of corporate America. Next Webb developed the Scales of Justice series, full of actresses playing attorneys wearing only suit jackets and stiletto heels and judges with surprises under their flowing robes.

Now, two decades and many movies later, Webb's business empire included a state-of-the-art production studio in Sarasota, an Internet website, and a distribution warehouse in Miami to fill the thousands of orders that poured in every month. He'd chosen to locate in Sarasota in part because he hated the cold northeast winters but also because he wanted the option of shooting outside all year round. The location had afforded him another rich stream of ideas. His Circus series was wildly successful, and Fishermen and Golfers were big hits as well. It was amazing how creative his actors could be with fishing rods and seven irons.

Webb was enthused about his latest project. *Velvet Nights in Venice*. He'd written the script, inspired by the Venetian architecture of Cà d'Zan and the velvety skin of Merilee. Tonight the plans were all in place to shoot on the terrace of the old Ringling mansion at a fund-raiser being held for literacy projects. What a joke! Brian Mueller would shoot video for Suncoast News Network, and all the society swells would be eager to have their mugs shown on the eleven o'clock news supporting the worthy cause. Little would they suspect that the outtakes would be used to open Webb's next video.

Mueller had his instructions. He would take care to get extra video of the guests taken from angles that didn't show their faces. He'd get lots of long shots and back shots of the gowned and tuxedoed partygoers clustered on the Italian marble terrace sipping cocktails and champagne on a warm summer night. The Boys Next Door would be playing, keeping everyone smiling. Festive material indeed to set the scene for the movie that would take off as two of the revelers steal away for a tryst in the side garden beneath the bronze statue of the naked babies Romulus and Remus with their wolf mother.

Of course, the core of the movie would be shot later. Merilee and Van would shoot that in the protected studio, and then the scenes of thrashing would be edited to the terrace party material to look as though it had all happened the same night. To make the transition seamless, Webb planned to have his stars mingling with all the aboveboard types during the cocktail hour. He'd spent a small fortune on Merilee's dress, but he hadn't minded one bit. He'd loved watching her model it for him last week. Her smooth shoulders gleamed over the strapless lamé gown. Her brown eyes sparkled as she twirled in delight, tossing her dark hair. She was a natural for this business, but as Webb viewed her in the designer attire, he knew that under a different set of circumstances, Merilee could make it in the respectable world as well. She carried herself with her chin raised, erect and graceful. There was soft Latin beauty to her face. It was just an accident of birth that had led Merilee to this line of work. An accident of birth and the fact that she had been in the wrong place at the wrong time.

But she sure wasn't dumb. When she found out how many copies her first video had sold, she was right in there, threatening to leave if Webb didn't give her a cut of the profits on the next one. No way that was ever going to happen.

Webb rose from the sofa, walked over to the wall unit, and took the video from the player. He needed to get dressed and drive to the office. He had to go to Plan B and get Gloria up to speed. Fortunately she was the same size as Merilee and could slip into the form-fitting gown.

Yes, Gloria would have to step into Merilee's role, because his beauty had been missing for several days now.

CHAPTER
12

Leroy Barry clicked through the Sarasota website looking for a place to use as a base of operation when they covered what he hoped would be a rip-roaring, raging hurricane. He had a list of criteria. First off, he wanted to be near something visual. The ocean was preferable, with a pier or jetty that the waves could crash on. Lots of swaying palm trees would be a plus as well.

But Leroy had special, technical concerns. The satellite truck they would be using had to be parked in a protected area. The camera set up for live shots should be kept dry. A hotel suite with sliding glass doors to the terrace would work fine for the latter concern. Cassie could go out on the terrace and get blown around in the wind and pounding rain while the cameraman, Felix Rodriguez, could shoot, nice and dry, from inside the room.

Leroy had been to Sarasota several times before. As he scrolled through the hotel listings, he remembered there was an inn with terraces and covered parking facing a marina on Sarasota Bay leading out to the Gulf of Mexico. Yeah, there it was. This should work out fine. All those boats tossing about in the angry waters would be just out their window. He dialed the number and booked two rooms on an upper floor and two downstairs, all facing the marina.

They had to get going on the drive across state. These tropical storms could turn into hurricanes even when the weather service wasn't really expecting them to. Giselle was gathering speed quickly, and Leroy didn't want to get caught with his pants down. And what did they have to do anyway? New York wasn't putting them on TV for anything else. If this kept up, someone up there might have the bright idea that there was no need for a Miami Bureau. For the umpteenth time Leroy resented the hell out of being saddled with Cassie Sheridan.

Go figure. Once, being Cassie's producer was one of the most prestigious spots for any of the *Evening Headlines* producers. Working with her ensured that your work would be regularly on air. You'd have a shot at Emmy and Peabody Awards. But no more. That was too bad for Cassie, but he had to make himself valued by the powers that be. He couldn't be tainted by his association with her.

Leroy clicked off the website and walked over to the next office. The correspondent was at her desk, frowning, watching a television monitor tuned to the Weather Channel. She looked up at Leroy as he stood in the doorway and waited for him to speak.

"Go home and pack your gear. We'll drive over to Sarasota this afternoon."

Cassie let out a sound, somewhere between a sigh and a groan.

Leroy's eyes narrowed behind his black-framed glasses. "Bad attitude, Cassie. I'd think you'd be eager to get out and try to get on the air. I know I damn well want to."

"I know you do, Leroy. And I feel for you. I do. We both know what's going on, though we don't talk about it."

He watched Cassie as her shoulders slumped. He might even have felt sorry for her, if his own fate weren't so entangled with hers. Instead, he felt angry at her defeatist attitude. "Look, I'm not interested in a lengthy discussion of what's going on with you and your career right now, Cassie. Let's just get out of this office and cover some news. Go ahead, go home and pack your boots and rubber pants."

Cassie got up, switched off the television, and hitched her carry bag onto her shoulder. Leroy stepped aside as she silently passed him on her way out the door.

How the mighty had fallen.

CHAPTER
13

Sarasota's elderly population ensured that J. Harrison Lewis, M.D., had a thriving practice. There was an endless supply of cloudy cataracts that needed to be removed, and Harry had the best reputation in the city for getting the job done. Business was so good that the wait for an initial appointment was two months, and surgeries were scheduled another month to six weeks after that.

Perhaps the wait wouldn't have been so long if Dr. Lewis had put in more working hours. But life was short, and what was the point of all those years in medical school and internship and residency and pushing himself at Manhattan Eye, Ear and Throat if now, after building his private practice here in the Sunshine State, he didn't enjoy the fruits of his labor? He instructed his nurses not to schedule anything after two o'clock, he took every Wednesday and weekend off, and he made a point of taking at least six weeks of vacation each year. He wanted to have time to enjoy the new boat he had bought, the boat he had christened *The Eyes Have It.* Sailing was his passion.

Harry was not really a people person, as his patients would say, while hastening to add that they didn't care if his bedside manner wasn't the best as long as his hands were steady and he knew what he was doing. In a world where a single man was a rare commodity, many women had tried to entice him.

"The actual surgery will take only about a half an hour, Mrs. Chambers, but you better plan to spend about three hours in the hospital. The anesthesiologist will make sure you are comfortable during the operation. You'll be awake during the surgery, but you won't feel any pain."

Etta gripped Charles's hand as they listened to what was to come.

Dr. Lewis didn't bother giving an understanding smile or reaching out to pat Etta's arm in a sign of reassurance. "My nurse tells me that we have a last-minute cancellation, so we have an opening tomorrow morning.

We could do the surgery then, or else you can wait until the end of September or early October. It's up to you."

The couple looked at each other. "Whatever you want to do, Etta," Charles said soothingly.

"Oh my, I wasn't prepared for this," said his wife. "But maybe it would be good to get it over with instead of worrying about it for the next month."

"Fine," declared the ophthalmologist, quickly making a notation in his book. "Tomorrow morning. Ten o'clock. Don't wear any makeup or jewelry or hairpins, and make sure to wear loose and comfortable clothing. Take any medication you normally take."

Dr. Lewis rose to dismiss his patient, extending his hand across the desk. "See you tomorrow."

Etta and Charles left the office, not quite knowing what had hit them, as the doctor rang for his nurse to bring him his lunch. As usual, he'd been up early to perform surgery, and he was hungry. He had fifteen minutes penciled in to eat before his next appointment. Just enough time to scarf down his chef's salad and catch the top of the noon news.

CHAPTER
14

"Hannah? Hi, honey. It's Mom."

"Oh, hi."

Cassie's heart sank at the lack of enthusiasm in her daughter's voice.

"How's everything going, sweetheart?"

"Fine."

"What have you been doing?"

"Not much."

"Have you been going to the pool?"

"Not really."

"Playing any softball?"

"The season's over, Mom," answered the thirteen-year-old with resignation. "Don't you know anything?" was left unspoken.

Cassie eyed the packed canvas duffel bag in her foyer as she twisted the telephone cord in her free hand. She didn't want to tell Hannah, but it would be worse if she waited. "How's the weather up there, Hannah?"

God, she sounded so lame. Like she was making polite small talk with a stranger. Not the conversation that a mother and daughter should be having.

"It's hot. Hot and muggy." Hannah sounded bored.

"That's the way it is down here, too." Cassie swallowed. "But there's a storm brewing off the western coast of the state. It's close to becoming a hurricane."

No response on the other end of the telephone line.

"Hannah?"

"Yeah?"

"Honey, I have to go to Sarasota, to be in place in case this thing turns into a hurricane."

"So?" Her daughter was going to make her say it.

"So I might not be able to come up there this weekend."

"Figures." The sarcasm in Hannah's tone stung.

"Oh, Hannah, please don't be like that. You know there's nothing I want more than to come up and see you." Cassie didn't like the pleading quality she heard in her voice.

"Yeah, Mom. Right."

"Hannah, I'm so sorry. But what can I do? You know how it is, honey. This is my job." Cassie wanted to add, the job that pays for all those trips to The Gap and J. Crew, but she held her tongue.

"Yeah, I know how it is, Mom. It's always your job."

Cassie cast around for a way to respond. Hannah had a point, and they both knew it. "Look, if I can't make it this weekend, I'll try for the following one."

"That won't work out, Mom. Daddy and I are going away that weekend."

"Oh, you are? Where?"

"Rehoboth."

Cassie's mind quickly made the connection. Gillian Cox, the principal at Jim's school, had a beach house in Rehoboth. In fact, Cassie and Jim and Hannah had visited there together in happier times. "Are you going to Mrs. Cox's place?"

"Um-hmm."

"Oh, that's nice." Cassie tried to be upbeat.

"I might as well tell you, Mom. Daddy and Mrs. Cox have been going out together." As she had been hurt, Hannah wanted to hurt her mother.

She succeeded.

CHAPTER
15

"Mom! Mom! I'm going to be on TV!" Vincent ran into the kitchen, panting. "Hurry up, turn it on!"

Wendy Bayler looked up from spreading peanut butter on Wonder bread, unable to respond before her son spun on his heels and scurried to the television set. She wiped her hands on a paper towel and followed Vincent into the tiny living room.

"Come on, Mom!" the boy urged. "There's going to be a story about me." He hoped she wouldn't realize that he should have asked her permission to be on the news. It was too late now.

Mark poked his small head out of the bedroom to see what the commotion was about. Wendy's first instinct was to tell her younger son to stay in the air-conditioned room, but the excitement on Vincent's face made her reconsider. For once in her sons' lives she didn't want the moment wrecked by the worries of that damned cystic fibrosis. For once they were going to live as she imagined other people lived and just enjoy the moment. She gathered her sons beside her on the worn couch and watched the opening of *The News at Noon.*

"Siesta Beach was the scene of a gruesome discovery this morning," announced the anchorman, "as a human hand was found by a Siesta Key boy. Suncoast News Reporter Tony Whitcomb has the story." Slack-jawed, Wendy turned to look at her older son, but Vincent was staring wide-eyed at the TV screen.

The reporter began his narration. "Most mornings, eleven-year-old Vincent Bayler combs the beach with his metal detector, looking for spare change and metallic treasures in the sand. But this morning was not like other mornings."

Vincent's flushed face popped up on the screen. "The metal detector went off over a clump of seaweed. I pulled back the seaweed and that's when I found it."

"What did you find?" asked the reporter.

"A hand."

Now Wendy wished that she had instructed Mark to stay in the bedroom. The five-year-old grabbed his mother's arm and let out a phlegmy cough.

"Sarasota Sherriff's Deputy Danny Gregg was the first officer to respond to the scene," continued the reporter's deep voice. Wendy recognized the policeman who had come to their house that night last year to help Mark.

"I called my supervisor, and detectives were dispatched to the scene," said the deputy. "The hand was taken downtown to the forensics lab, where our experts will conduct their investigation. They'll try to get fingerprints, and we'll be checking for any missing persons reported within the past few weeks."

"But," the reporter continued, "clear fingerprints may be hard to obtain. Vincent Bayler says the hand was in poor condition."

"It was all bloated and raggedy and it looked like the fish had gotten at it," the boy described with a little too much enthusiasm. "Maybe even sharks!"

The reporter appeared on the screen now, standing on the sand with the Gulf of Mexico lapping behind him. "Police say this does *not* appear to be a shark attack. They told Suncoast News that the wrist had been cleanly severed. Tony Whitcomb, Suncoast News Network, on Siesta Beach."

Vincent looked up expectantly at his mother. "Cool, huh?"

"No, Vincent, it is not cool. It's horrible." Wendy's brow furrowed as she looked at her son. She worried about this kid of hers. Was it a normal boy thing that he looked at finding a human hand this way as a source of excitement? Yet she supposed it was better that Vincent viewed this nightmare as an adventure rather than being traumatized by it.

Her thoughts were distracted by the sound of Mark's cough. "Come on, big guy," she urged, putting her arms beneath Mark's and boosting him up. "Get back into your room, and I'll bring in your lunch on a tray."

"Will you stay with me while I eat, Mommy?"

"Yes, I will. Now go ahead, Mark. Get in there."

When the boy had shut the bedroom door behind him, Wendy turned to her other child. "Explain something to me, Vincent. I don't understand why the metal detector went off."

Vincent arranged a look of innocence on his freckled face. "Whaddya mean?"

"I mean, a hand doesn't have any metal in it. Why would a metal detector go off?"

CHAPTER
16

In his cluttered office at the marina, Jerry watched *The News at Noon,* paying close attention to the weather report at the end. Pointing to his blue-and-green electronic map, the meteorologist said that Tropical Storm Giselle was heading in their general direction. Suncoast News was keeping a close watch on Giselle, the weatherman reassured his audience, and would keep Sarasotans apprised of the latest developments.

"Of course, folks, we don't want anyone to panic, but you must be prepared. Locate your evacuation zone. You can find it printed in the front of your phone book. Check out your evacuation route and the shelters near you and practice driving to them. And remember, be flexible. It's impossible to tell in advance which roads may be closed."

Jerry Dean let out a low groan as he walked out to the dock and surveyed the boats bobbing gently in the green water. He had close to two hundred boats in his marina. Many of them were owned by locals, some were owned by people from outside the state who used them when they came down to vacation. All would have to be secured as tightly as possible to survive whipping winds and surging water. Jerry knew that, despite his best efforts, if the storm hit them hard, they were going to sustain big losses.

The marina owner had been down this road before. When the last big storm blew through, owners had little time to secure their boats, leaving dozens to sink or suffer major damage. High winds tore sailboats from their moorings, tossing them like bath toys in the choppy water and smashing them into the Ringling Causeway, banging them over and over again against the bridge until their masts collapsed. Predictably, too many of his customers blamed Jerry for their losses. After that storm some owners moved their boats elsewhere. It had taken the last three years to get business back to where it had been before. Only the surreptitious renting of clients' boats had helped him make it through.

As he squinted out into the clear horizon, it was hard to believe that another violent storm was brewing out there, steadily growing, heading his way. Jerry took off his orange baseball cap and wiped the perspiration from his creased brow. The days of preparation were going to be long ones. Maybe the storm would fizzle out, but he wasn't going to be caught unprepared this time.

The office telephone rang, and Jerry went back inside to grab it. "Marina."

"Jerry? It's Webb Morelle. Just checking that everything is on for tonight."

"Yeah, Webb. Your boat's all fueled up and ready to go."

"Great, guy. Thanks. And you're still on to take us up there?"

The last thing Jerry needed right now was to waste his time chauffeuring Webb and his wife to that charity bash up at Cà d'Zan, but Webb was a good customer who always paid his bills on time and Jerry didn't want to break his promise. "Yep. All set."

"Good, because Lou-Anne has a hankering to arrive by boat and make her grand entrance up that big ole marble staircase at the Ringling dock. I don't want to disappoint her, buddy."

"I understand, Webb." Jerry tried to keep the weariness out of his voice. "You said six o'clock, right?"

"Yeah, be ready at six—but if I know Lou-Anne, we'll be late."

"I'll be here."

Jerry was about to hang up, but he heard Webb continue to speak. "And, Jerry, just to let you know, I think we'll be bringing a couple of guests along."

"Whatever you want, Webb. Whatever you want."

CHAPTER
17

The hand on Siesta Beach was hers. It was Merilee's. He was sure of it.

The anxious feelings that had boiled within him over many years were relieved by forcing himself on his victims and, once his energy was spent, walking away. He had done lots of things. Horrible things. Brutal things. But he had never killed before. He had never meant to kill Merilee.

He had seen her in her movies, and he knew this depraved life wasn't the life she was meant to live. Perhaps she hadn't realized it yet, but her relationship with him would have set her free. And he was sure that she would have set him free as well. If he could have had a real relationship with her, he'd hoped he wouldn't have had to go on doing what he had done to those other girls.

Merilee had been interested enough in him, in his plans for them together, that she had gone out with him on the boat that night, into the dark waters of the Gulf. It had been going so well. She had been delighted with the ring, smiling in the moonlight when he slipped it on her finger.

He hadn't been able to help himself. He'd been so excited he just had to do it, just for a few minutes, just to relax. He'd excused himself and gone to the head. But he stayed in there too long, painting the blue around his eyes, powdering his face. He had planned to wipe it all off before he went up to her again, but he didn't have the chance.

If only she hadn't come below and opened the door. If only she hadn't seen him, and mocked him. If only she could have loved him the way he needed to be loved.

He couldn't bear to see her running away from him, scrambling up the ladder to the deck. He followed her, wanting to explain, wanting to make it all right between them again. But up on the deck Merilee would have none of him; she demanded that he take her back to shore. "Get away from me, you sick freak."

Her words still echoed in his mind.

He'd lashed out, striking her across her beautiful face. She fell backward, hitting her head against the railing. Dazed, yet still repelled by him, she pushed him away as he tried to wrap his arms around her.

All the rage that he felt, rage that had grown over years of derision and self-loathing, seethed within him, culminated in the heave that sent her over the side of the boat.

When he revved the motor, he heard a thud. He felt sick as he imagined the propeller slicing at her beautiful body.

Maybe he had set her free after all. Yes, Merilee was free now. Free from the sick life she had been living. But he was left behind, still shackled by his desperate desires. And, once again, the media were covering the results of his actions.

He needed some release. He thought of the nurse. He'd had his eyes on her for a while now. The pretty one he'd noticed when he went to visit the kids in the pediatric unit at the hospital. She had been so appreciative of his coming to entertain the sick children.

He'd taken to waiting in the parking lot to catch a glimpse of her when she left at the end of her shift. Once, he'd followed her into the supermarket where she stopped on the way home. He'd purposely bumped his cart into hers, then apologized profusely. She'd shown no recognition—hadn't known him without his clown makeup. Nor had she shown any interest in him. But she'd liked him with the makeup, he thought with hope.

He didn't like the idea of striking where he lived. It was better to do it out of town, but it would probably be a few more months before he had the opportunity to leave Sarasota. He didn't know if he could wait that long.

CHAPTER
18

He was pretty sure his mother had bought his hastily concocted explanation that the metal detector must have been triggered by a bottle cap that happened to be lying next to the hand. For once Vincent was glad about Mark's coughing fit. It distracted his mother from questioning him further.

"I'm going out, Mom," he called into the bedroom. Vincent grabbed his peanut-butter-and-jelly sandwich and headed to the beach. He found Gideon out on the Old Pier.

"They biting?" asked Vincent, taking a seat on the concrete wall.

The fisherman thrust his chin in the direction of his empty bucket. "Nah. Caught a couple of catfish, but I threw 'em back."

Vincent nodded, knowing that Gideon wanted the good stuff. Pompano was his favorite. Permit, a close second. The boy riffled through the worn tacklebox, examining Gideon's treasured lures.

The fisherman put fresh bait on his hook. "Did you see yourself on the news?"

"Yep."

"Your mother see you?"

"Yep."

"What did she say?"

"She wanted to know why my metal detector went off when a hand doesn't have any metal in it."

Gideon cast the fishing line into the rolling water. "Good question. I guess the police will get around to wondering about that, too."

The boy was silent as he digested the thought.

"Anything you feel like telling me, Vincent?"

"Yeah, I guess so." He pulled the ruby ring out of the pocket of his shorts and handed it up to Gideon.

CHAPTER
19

Alligator Alley was aptly named, thought Cassie as she gazed out the car window at the canal that ran alongside the highway. Scores of alligators, lethal giants trying to retain heat from the sun, stretched out on the banks. Mammoth, black birds hung motionless with wings spread wide in the limbs of the trees that dotted the landscape, looking like huge bats. The scene was surreal, and Cassie gave an involuntary shudder.

"Anhingas," said Leroy, breaking the silence that had enveloped them since they'd gotten into the Jeep in Miami. Felix was following in the satellite truck.

"What?"

"Those birds are called anhingas. They dive into the water for their food, and they sit in the trees with their wings spread open like that to dry out."

"They're creepy looking. Gruesome really," Cassie answered. She had no desire to keep the conversation going. She continued to stare out the window, watching as one alligator slid from the bank into the murky water and another opened his vicious snout as if yawning. As the car carried her farther and farther from Miami, the knot in Cassie's stomach grew tighter.

So, the widowed Mrs. Cox and the soon to be divorced Jim Sheridan were seeing each other. That was just great. It wouldn't have hurt as much if Gillian Cox weren't such a nice person. Cassie liked the school principal very much. She was smart, good at her job, had a great sense of humor, and was pretty, too. Of course Jim would be attracted to her. Cassie tortured herself, imagining Hannah at a beachside seafood restaurant, cracking her favorite lobster claws and laughing with her father and Gillian Cox. Sitting at the table where Cassie should have been. Gillian Cox standing in as Hannah's mother.

Oh God, what am I doing? she asked herself silently as the car sped across the baking asphalt. With every fiber of her being, she wanted not to be going on this trip.

CHAPTER
20

Anthony walked on short, bandy legs across the hot, concrete parking lot next to the circus museum. He was scheduled to do the two o'clock tour, and he liked to arrive ahead of time. Today he was running behind. He'd been helping out with the preparations for the party tonight. His mother would enjoy seeing what was going on over at the mansion, just a couple hundred yards away. They were really doing it up over there.

If you were going to do something, you might as well do it right. That's what his mother had always told him. He loved his mother, and he knew that from the moment she realized the child to whom she had given birth was going to have an especially tough row to hoe, she had worked to prepare him to have the best life he possibly could.

Mother didn't feel sorry for him or, if she did, she didn't show it. She encouraged him to study hard, play sports, have friends, though that wasn't easy. Kids were afraid of anyone who was different, and they expressed their fears in mean taunts and ostracism. But Anthony had learned early on that, while his mother would dry his tears, she wouldn't allow her son to isolate himself. She'd send him right back out to the playground again. He was going to have to learn to live in the world as it was. A world populated by a lot of so-called normal people who thought that "little people" were some kind of sideshow for their amusement.

Anthony noticed a familiar bicycle propped against the wall on the side of the museum building. Sure enough, Vincent was waiting at the doorway. "You here again?" Anthony asked, shaking his head but smiling.

Vincent's head bobbed up and down. "Anthony! You'll never guess what happened!"

Anthony looked past the boy to the small crowd gathered at the reception desk. "I want to hear all about it, kid, but it'll have to wait until after the tour."

The boy was always riding his bike all the way up here, enthralled by everything to do with the circus. Anthony had lost count of the times he had guided Vincent through the museum along with the paying customers. After the first couple of tours, Anthony had told him that he could come along for free. He wasn't sure if that had been a mistake or not. The kid couldn't get enough. He should be out playing with other kids on these summer afternoons. Instead, he was spending them in a museum that he had already been through so many times he could probably have given a good tour himself. Still, Anthony understood Vincent's fascination. He shared it.

"Sarasota's honeymoon with 'The Greatest Show on Earth' lasted for thirty-three years as the Ringling Brothers and Barnum and Bailey Circus wintered here from 1927 to 1960," Anthony began as his tour group gathered around him. "Each season as it traveled across the country, the circus pro-moted Sarasota as Florida's most beautiful city, which led thousands of tourists to come here for a behind-the-scenes look at the big show."

The group shuffled from room to room, looking and listening as Anthony described the activities and logistics of the circus. He peppered his descriptions with the words as-sociated with the circus. "*Clown* originally meant 'clod,' and the word was used to de-note a clumsy country bumpkin," Anthony explained as the group examined the life casts, plaster replicas of the talented clowns' faces. "But as P. T. Barnum said, 'Ele-phants and clowns are the pegs on which the circus is hung.'"

Anthony took care to explain the three types of clowns. "The whiteface clown is meant to play straight man to the Auguste, the clown with the most comic face. The Au-guste is considered the prankster among clowns. And, of course, there is also the character clown, the most recognizable of which are the tramps or the hobos."

"Like Emmett Kelly?" someone asked.

"Exactly," answered Anthony.

Vincent and his group listened to Anthony's stories of the Flying Wallendas and rubbed the sides of the silver truck mounted with a gigantic cannon that shot human beings into the air. "The mechanism in the truck is a guarded family secret," whispered the diminutive docent.

After describing the difference between Asian and African elephants—"the easiest way to tell are the ears; the African ears are sometimes four feet wide, the Asian ears are much smaller"—Anthony took his group past the carved tiger cages and organs and calliopes into the last large room, rimmed with old wooden circus wagons. In the middle of the room a miniature, automated circus had been built to scale. Anthony said good-bye, leaving the circus enthusiasts to ooh and aah over the tiny mechanical ringmaster and flying trapeze artists.

"I don't know about you, kid, but I'm thirsty. Let's go get something to drink." The little man and the boy walked outside to the screened restaurant that sat in the shade of a huge banyan tree. Finally, as they waited for the waitress to come and take their order, Vincent had his chance to describe what had happened that morning.

Anthony let out a thin whistle from between his teeth.

"And I was on TV, too!" the boy continued
with enthusiasm.

"Sorry I missed it."

"Oh, I think it might be on again tonight,"
Vincent offered. "You can see it then."

Anthony nodded, but Vincent suspected
his friend was thinking about something else
as he watched Anthony's eyes staring toward Cà d'Zan.

"Hey, Anthony," the boy said, trying to pull
back his friend's attention, "will you give me
that makeup lesson today?"

"Another time, Vincent. I can't do it now. I
have to get to the hospital. Those kids are
waiting to see their favorite clown."

The boy was disappointed, but he shook it
off. He would ride down to the marina and
hang around there for a while.

CHAPTER
21

This ring was too good to go to his usual guy out on the Tamiami Trail. This required a trip to posh St. Armands Circle, and Gideon knew he had better go all out in his preparation. He shaved the three-day-old stubble from his weathered face, trimmed his mustache, clipped his fingernails, and combed back his white hair from his suntanned brow. He pulled on his one pair of nice trousers and buttoned on a collared sports shirt, sliding the ring into the breast pocket.

With trepidation he drove his old Plymouth across the Ringling Causeway. It was obvious the ring was worth a lot of money. But it was also evidence in a police investigation, and he knew he shouldn't be trying to sell it. Gideon's lips moved as he talked to himself, trying to rationalize what he was about to do.

Vincent was a good kid, and his mother was a decent woman who was struggling to keep her little family together. They could sure use the money the ring would bring. If the ring was turned over to the cops, it might help identify the hand, but it wouldn't do a thing to help Vincent and, after all, the boy had found it. Finders keepers. Let the cops do their jobs some other way.

Gideon drove around the circle twice before finding a parking space. He didn't bother to lock the rickety old car. If someone wanted to steal a car, there were lots of nicer ones than his to choose from among the BMWs and Mercedes lining the curb. He walked past the high-end boutiques and gift shops until he reached his destination. The icy air inside Sebastien Jewelers was welcoming after the oppressive heat on the sidewalk. A well-groomed man was bent into the display window, removing glittering necklaces and bracelets. "Can I help you, sir?" asked the man, eyeing Gideon's clothing.

Gideon was keenly aware that he was out of place here. A fish out of water. "Yes. I have a ring I'd like you to take a look at."

"Certainly, sir. Please, come over here."

The jeweler gestured to the counter at the side of the store. A blue velvet pad sat on top of the sparkling glass. With his callused hand, Gideon pulled the ring from his pocket and placed it on the pad. The jeweler picked it up, turned it in his hand to examine it, then held it up in the air, where the rubies caught the light. "This a beautiful ring, sir. Very beautiful."

"What is it worth?"

Leslie Sebastien knew exactly what it was worth. He had designed and sold it. The question was, where had this old guy gotten it?

CHAPTER
22

In her room at the Inn by the Bay, Cassie didn't bother unpacking. It didn't make sense to put things in the dresser drawers when there was the distinct possibility that they might have to check out quickly and change locations. Best just to pull things out of her duffel bag as she needed them. She did, however, hang up a few shirts and the yellow slicker she had brought and threw her rubber boots into the bottom of the closet. Glamour clothes.

Kicking off her shoes, she instinctively switched on the television set, clicking the remote control until she found the KEY affiliate. She still had some time to kill before the local six o'clock news began, and she could get the lowdown on how the area was gearing up for Giselle. She dialed down for room service, ordering some wine along with her turkey club. Let Leroy and Felix go to that restaurant on St. Armands Circle that Leroy had been raving about. Cassie had no desire to join them for dinner.

She flopped down on the king-size bed and picked up the telephone. On the off chance that the attorney representing her might still be in his office, Cassie dialed the number for the KEY News legal department in New York.

"Glenn Jones."

"It's Cassie Sheridan, Glenn, just checking to see if there's anything new." Like a little kid, she found herself squeezing her eyes shut and crossing the fingers of her free hand.

"Look, Cassie, we talked about this, didn't we? These things take time. Stop worrying, will you?"

The lawyer was right about the time part. The pretrial antics had been dragging on for months as Cassie and KEY News lost their motions on getting the suit dismissed for one reason or another. "Easy for you to say, Glenn. You'll still have your job and your house no matter how this suit turns out."

In addition to being a crackerjack attorney, Glenn was a good hand holder, adept at soothing his clients' frayed nerves. "Yes, you're right. I will have my job because we are going to win this case. Anyone can file a suit about anything, Cassie. On our side is the fact that Pamela Lynch is a public figure. That makes her fair game for the report you gave. We've talked about all this before."

"But her daughter wasn't a public figure," Cassie said. "Maggie Lynch was just a young woman who had the misfortune of not only being raped but having the event broadcast on the national news. She couldn't take it."

Glenn's tone was serious. "Cut it out,

Cassie. As your attorney and as your friend, I'm telling you, stop feeling sorry for yourself, and stop blaming yourself. If we can't settle this thing and we end up in court, you are going to be called on to testify. You better get your head on straight. You reported the news. Nothing more."

Cassie didn't respond.

"Okay." Glenn filled the void patiently. "It might have been better if you hadn't said her name. Reporting the name of a rape victim can be actionable. But we can argue that even if you hadn't mentioned Maggie Lynch by name, people would have figured out who you meant. Pamela Lynch has only one daughter. If that daughter was the reason the FBI director named someone to the Fugitives List, the public has a right to know that."

To hear Glenn tell it, it made sense. Cassie listened as the attorney continued. "The company has to stick with you, Cassie. First of all, one of their executives, namely Range, forced the story on the air. Second, this could set a bad precedent for all media firms, scaring them off stories and leaving them much more vulnerable to lawsuits. There are some First Amendment issues here, and KEY needs to fight this case and win."

"Okay," she answered, mollified for the time being. "You'll keep me posted on what's happening?"

"Promise. Where are you, anyway?"

"In Sarasota, Florida, waiting for a hurricane."

"Swell. Well, hang in there, Cassie, and stop worrying. We have things under control up here."

As she placed the receiver back into the cradle, there was a knock on the door. Cassie got up and grabbed her purse, taking out a few singles for the waiter with her room service tray. Heading straight for the red wine, she filled her glass and took a generous swallow, followed by another. Pointing the remote at the television, she raised the volume and watched the story of the little kid who had found a human hand on the beach that morning.

The turkey sandwich lay untouched on its plate, but the wine had all been swallowed when the phone rang. "Cassie, it's me. Leroy."

"Hi." What did he want now?

"I just heard that the Boys Next Door are playing on the grounds of the old Ringling estate tonight. I called and, no surprise, they want all the publicity they can get. It's never enough for these guys. Let's go."

"Come on, Leroy." Cassie was exasperated. "You know damn well we won't be airing that on KEY. It's just another concert. There's no news in that, no matter how big the band is."

"Yeah, I know that and you know that. But *they* don't know that. It'll be fun. We'll go through the motions of shooting something, and then we can eat, drink, and be merry. And, if it will make you happy, I'll pitch it to *KEY to America.*"

"I didn't know you were a fan of the Boys Next Door," she said. "I thought boy bands appealed to my thirteen-year-old daughter and her friends, not to grown men." Could she try any harder to alienate Leroy?

He ignored the slight. "Get ready. We'll meet down in the lobby in fifteen minutes."

CHAPTER
23

A welcome breeze blew in from the bay, cooling the guests gathered on the mottled marble terrace at Cà d'Zan. There was some major league wealth assembled here tonight, thought Cassie, observing the designer gowns and heavy jewelry. She fingered the platinum wedding band, channeled with diamonds, that she still wore on her left ring finger. She supposed she should stop wearing it, but tonight she was glad that she hadn't taken it off yet. Dressed in black pants and a T-shirt, she was self-conscious, but she had come to Sarasota to cover a hurricane, not a society party.

A thirty-something man approached the KEY crew. His white linen shirt was opened almost to his belt buckle. Heavy gold chains were spread across his chest hair. Suddenly, Cassie felt better about her own attire.

Leroy shook hands with Sarge Tucker and made the rest of the introductions. "This is our correspondent, Cassie Sheridan, and our cameraman, Felix Rodriguez."

"Nice to meet you. Glad you came," said the band promoter, pumping Cassie's hand enthusiastically. "The boys are ready for a great show."

"So, how is it that the band is playing here?" asked Cassie.

"Sarasota's my hometown," answered Sarge. "They only have one more concert on this tour, scheduled for Tampa tomorrow night. We were able to fit this stop in because it's so close and because I asked them to do it for me. These guys have hearts of gold. So, anyway, make yourselves at home and let me know if there's anything I can do for you while you're here tonight."

"As a matter of fact, there *is* something I'd like to ask you for, if it's not too much trouble," said Cassie, thinking the night shouldn't be a total loss. "My daughter, Hannah, is a big Boys Next Door fan. Any chance I can get an autographed picture of the band for her?"

"Sure thing," Sarge answered. "I'll be sure to get you one by the end of the evening."

*　*　*

Etta was glad she had volunteered to staff the reception desk. She wanted to be busy and keep her mind off the upcoming surgery. After she had checked off the arriving guests, she planned to excuse herself, drive home, and get to bed early. With a little luck, if the surgery went well, this might be the last time that driving after dark would be worrisome for her. Dr. Lewis said that after the operation the night lights of the highway shouldn't bother her anymore.

Think of the devil. Dr. Lewis stood before her, looking quite dashing in his tuxedo. Etta craned her neck to look for his escort. She didn't see one. "Good evening, Dr. Lewis."

By the blank expression on his face, Etta realized that the doctor didn't place her. She was a bit hurt but quickly rationalized. He had hundreds of patients. How could he remember all of them? Just as long as he recognized her tomorrow morning in the operating room. "Etta Chambers, Dr. Lewis. You're doing my cataracts tomorrow."

"Oh, yes, of course, Etta. Good to see you." He didn't bother trying to make any more small talk. Once his name was marked off the guest list, he turned and left.

Etta was tempted to stay and keep an eye on how much the doctor drank. She didn't want a surgeon with a hangover slicing into her eyes in the morning.

"You clean up nice, fella. You didn't have to get all dressed up just to drive us up here."

"No problem, Webb."

"I don't know how long we'll be here, Jerry. You don't mind sticking around, do you, buddy?"

I don't have much choice, do I? thought the marina owner as he helped his passengers off the boat. Instead he answered, "No, Webb, I don't mind. I'll be waiting here for you whenever you all are ready to leave."

"And, Jerry, I found baby powder all over the floor of the head. You're not letting anyone else use my boat, are you, big fella?"

"No, of course not, Webb. If it got around that I let people use my customers' boats, I wouldn't have much of a marina." Jerry offered the first thing that came into his head. "Maybe something just fell out of the cabinet."

Webb was not mollified. "My kids have been out of diapers for quite a while now. I don't keep powder in the cabinet. And don't forget, Jerry," he said, turning away. "I decide who to loan my boat to."

Jerry watched the backs of Webb and Lou-Anne and the other couple, introduced to him as Gloria and Van, as they ascended the steps from the dock to the terrace at the back of the recently refurbished Cà d'Zan. Jerry already knew Van; the guy had recently contracted to dock his boat at the marina. The woman, Gloria, sure was stacked.

The lights inside the Mediterrean Gothic–style mansion shone through the pastel-colored leaded glass windows, bathing the bedecked party guests in a flattering glow. It was quite a scene, Jerry thought, like something out of a movie.

Jerry saw Webb stop to talk to a guy lugging a big camera and watched as Webb pointed to Gloria. The man hoisted the camera to his shoulder and pointed it in the direction of the shiny gold dress.

Jerry climbed back onboard the boat and opened the cooler he had stashed in the hold. Pulling out a Budweiser, he flipped the top and settled back to wait until he could go up there and get some of the good stuff. Why should he be the only one not drinking champagne?

* * *

Gloria reveled in making her entrance up the grand marble steps. She was so glad Merilee was out of the picture tonight. Now Gloria could be the belle of the ball. She felt like Cinderella in her shimmering golden gown, and she could tell she was making an impression by the heads, both male and female, that turned in her direction.

"You're knockin 'em dead, sweetheart," Van whispered in her ear. "You're absolutely glowing." Her escort squeezed her arm too hard.

Yes, Cinderella was a good comparison, she thought. Gloria had been feeling like a scullery maid since Merilee had become Webb's little pet. Merilee had been getting all the attention. Gloria had grown sick and tired of being second banana.

She smiled and laughed and sipped champagne from a fluted glass, aware that Brian Mueller was training his camera on her. Gloria wanted to shine in the video Brian was taking of her, knowing that these would be the opening shots for *Velvet Nights in Venice,* the movie that would get her career back on track. Gloria nuzzled Van's neck for the camera's benefit.

"Nice touch, baby," said Van.

"My pleasure." She smiled up at him.

She supposed Van Jensen had been a friend. He was rooting for Gloria, and he told her so, often. Though Merilee and Van had steamy chemistry on the set, they'd never seemed to get along when they put their clothes back on. Van didn't seem at all upset that Merilee was missing.

Gloria valued loyalty. She took Van's hand and decided that when they shot the hot scenes that were to be the meat of *Velvet Nights in Venice,* she wouldn't just go through the motions. She was going to show Van her appreciation and make sure he had an especially good time.

He really was Superman, Brian congratulated himself, serving two masters at the same time. Brian shot his pictures at every possible opportunity while letting Tony think he was shooting only for the SNN piece.

"Hey, did you see who's over there?" Tony was ogling. "That's Cassie Sheridan from KEY News."

Brian made no comment.

"I'm going to introduce myself."

Good, thought Brian, *now I can get some more stuff for Webb.*

While Felix, at Leroy's instruction, was per-functorily shooting some video, Cassie helped herself to the passing trays of shrimp, skewered chicken, and quiche. As she reached for another piece of shrimp, a man beside her commented on her ring. "That's a beauty."

"Why, thank you."

"I should know, I'm a jeweler. Leslie Se-bastien," said the man, extending his hand.

Cassie switched her glass to her left hand and shook his right one. "Cassie Sheridan."

"You look somehow familiar," he said, star-ing at her.

"I'm with KEY News."

He nodded and smiled. "Nice to meet you."

Cassie anticipated the conversation pro-gressing, but before either of them could go any further, a hand tapped Leslie Sebastien on his shoulder. "Excuse me, will you?" he asked and turned away.

Cassie shrugged and went to get another glass of wine.

*   *   *

Though she hadn't been thrilled when Webb told her he was bringing Gloria and Van along tonight, once her husband had reassured her that it would all look aboveboard, Lou-Anne Morelle hadn't protested too much. If she wanted to keep the lifestyle to which she had so happily become accustomed, she had to make a concession or two. And, after all, it was Gloria, not Merilee, that Webb had said would star in his next movie, and Lou-Anne was grateful for that. She hadn't liked Merilee from the first time she met the raven-haired beauty at Webb's office. But Webb was crazy about her. Too crazy.

Lou-Anne made it a point to talk to as many people as she could on the terrace. That was her job as a fund-raiser committee member. She knew, or at least recognized, most of the guests. It was the same crowd that attended all the other Sarasota social and charity events through the year. But what was with the woman standing by the bar wearing the black pants and T-shirt? For just an instant, Lou-Anne wrinkled her nose in distaste. The woman was surely pretty enough, but how gauche of her to come to this event dressed that way.

The small courtyard at the side of the house was a good place to talk. The two took a seat beneath the elevated bronze statues of the fabled Romulus and Remus.

"I'm sure it was the ring you bought," the jeweler insisted. "It was one of a kind. If there was any doubt, my hallmark stamped inside nailed it."

"What about the guy who brought it in?"

"I didn't recognize him," said Sebastien, "and he wouldn't leave his name. But I can tell you one thing. He hadn't been in the store before. This guy is no regular to St. Armands Circle."

"What did he look like?"

"Older guy, big, white mustache. Could be distinguished if he had the right clothes. Leathery skin, but not from sailing around on some yacht or golfing the fairways. This man works with his hands."

"Did you buy the ring from him?"

"No. I said it was getting late and I had somewhere to be. I thought I would talk to you first. I told him to come back tomorrow. I can have the police waiting for him then." Sebastien looked at his companion.

"Have you called the police already?"

"No. I wanted to see how you wanted to handle this. I didn't know if you wanted the police to be involved since you bought the ring for her."

"Let me think about it, will you, Leslie? I'll let you know before we leave tonight."

It was not the usual frenzied screaming that greeted the Boys Next Door as they ran out and took their places on the specially erected platform on the front lawn of Cà d'Zan, but the guests did applaud heartily.

"Hello, Sarasota," called Sarge Tucker into his microphone. "The Boys Next Door are honored to be here tonight to support the various wonderful charities in this, my beloved, hometown. Thank you, ladies and gents."

There was more enthusiastic applause as Sarge continued. "We have a special treat tonight. The boys are going to play, for the very first time before an audience, their new single—a song that is destined for the top of the charts. So, everybody, without further

ado, I present to you the Boys Next Door
and 'Nobody Knows.'"

The group bounded up to the stage, music blasting from the amplifiers placed strate-
gically around the mansion grounds, as
Sarge Tucker, gold chains flapping, jogged
off the stage. "Nobody Knows" seemed to
Cassie to be similar to the other Boys Next
Door songs she had heard repeatedly blar-
ing from Hannah's boom box. They had an-
noyed her then. Now she would give
anything to be upstairs in the Alexandria
house again, trying to block out the loud music.

"Don't look so enthused," shouted a voice
in her ear. It was Sarge Tucker, smiling and
holding out a glossy eight-by-ten. "For your
daughter," he offered. "I hope that's how
Hannah spells her name."

"Oh, yes, she'll be so thrilled. Thank you."
She arranged a pleasant expression on her
face and took the autographed picture from
him, feeling somewhat guilty. Cassie
doubted he would be so friendly if he realized that the video they had taken tonight
wouldn't air on KEY News.

The promoter held out his business card.

"Don't hesitate to call me if you need anything."

Cassie politely tucked the card into her purse.

She was going to call a taxi. Let Leroy and Felix stay as long as they cared to. She wanted to get out of here, go back to the hotel and go to bed. Too bad her heart wasn't into socializing. There were some very handsome men at this party, she thought as she stared at a particularly good-looking man, dashing in his tuxedo. As if he felt her eyes on him, he turned and lifted his champagne glass in a gentle salute.

Embarrassed, Cassie walked back to the bar on the terrace. Pulling her cell phone from her purse, she called information and scribbled the cab company's number on a cocktail napkin. Her next call told her that it would be twenty minutes before a car could pick her up. She asked the bartender for another glass of Merlot while she waited.

As she sipped the wine by herself, she couldn't help but listen to the loud conversation of the threesome that stood beside her.

"My God, that was Merilee's song," said the woman in the gold lamé gown. "I *know* that was it. If she was here, she'd be steaming."

"What do you mean, that was Merilee's song?" asked the swarthy tuxedo standing next to the gold lamé.

"She wrote that song, Van. I know. Merilee played 'Nobody Knows' for me months ago. Haven't you noticed how she's always working on her music between takes?"

The swarthy one shrugged. "I never paid much attention."

The woman turned to the other man. "Can't you do something about it, Webb? It's not fair. Merilee wrote that song, and now the Boys Next Door are going to make a fortune on it."

"Merilee's a big girl, Gloria. If there's a battle to be fought, she can fight it on her own. She doesn't need me or you or anyone else to do it for her. I don't want to get involved. Web of Desire doesn't need that kind of publicity."

The woman pushed back her teased hair. "Well, Merilee can't fight if she's not around to do the fighting. Don't get me wrong, Webb, I'm glad that I'm getting the chance to star in *Velvet Nights* since Merilee is AWOL, but while she's missing, I think, as a busi-

nessman, you should find out what she's en-
titled to for writing that song."

As if sensing a silent partner in their conversation, the man called Webb looked in
Cassie's direction. She felt her face grow
warm as she was caught eavesdropping.
She took the last sip of her wine, picked up
her purse from the bar, and walked away.

In the absence of anything else, a glass
would do it. It was a perfect murder weapon
because so many people were walking
around with one. A simple glass, taken from
the caterer's tray. A broken glass with a long,
sharp edge would do the trick.

"Leslie, can I talk to you again? Let's walk
over to the rose garden where the music
won't be so loud."

The jeweler came along readily, trustingly.
A lamb to the slaughter. Baa, baa, baa.

"So what do you want me to do? Should I
call the police and have them waiting when
the old guy comes back tomorrow?" asked
Sebastien. They walked past the statues of
smiling cherubs playing musical instruments
that lined the concrete drive leading to the
garden.

"What time did you tell him to come?"

"I told him to come back after five o'clock. Just after closing time."

They entered the garden, and the jeweler pulled a slim cigar from his jacket pocket. "I have another. Care to join me?"

"No thanks."

Sebastien took a seat on a garden bench. His face was briefly illuminated as he lit up and puffed.

Poor bastard.

"I'm in a bit of an awkward position here, Leslie. I really am in an awkward position. You understand, don't you?"

"Of course." The jeweler sat, staring straight ahead, working on his cigar while his companion paced.

"I really don't want the police to be called on this because I didn't want anyone to know I bought that ring, remember, Les?"

"Yes, I remember. And you have my word, I haven't told anyone that you did."

"Thank you, Les. I appreciate that. That's why I like doing business with you."

The pacing figure took a final swallow of champagne, walked behind the bench, and put one hand on the jeweler's tuxedoed shoulder while the other smashed the glass flute against the concrete bench. Leslie Sebastien looked up with surprise, and then alarm, as the crystal shard was jammed into his jugular vein.

TUESDAY

August 20

CHAPTER
24

Cassie hadn't requested a wake-up call because her body clock was programmed. The digital clock on the bedside table read 6:16. Her dry mouth and burning eyes told Cassie right away that she had had too much to drink the night before. She rose from the bed and stumbled into the bathroom, squinting as she switched on the overhead light. The mirror was unforgiving.

Splashing cold water on her face, she decided that she would force herself to go for her run. That would help cleanse her system. Listening to the Weather Channel, she pulled on shorts and a baggy T-shirt and tied up her running shoes. Giselle was now officially a hurricane, having gathered speed overnight. Winds in the Gulf were being clocked at up to 90 miles per hour. But it still wasn't clear if Sarasota would be the place Giselle made landfall.

Briefly, Cassie thought of leaving a message for Leroy, but she decided not to bother. She'd be back in less than an hour, and she doubted Leroy would be wanting to get an early start. He had been putting the drinks away pretty well, too, last night.

The sky was a soft gray color as she walked out of the hotel and did a few stretching exercises. She chose to turn right and started to jog, quickly reaching the Ringling Causeway. As she picked up speed, she passed early morning fishermen casting their lines over the causeway railing. The air was thick, and her breathing was labored. She had to lay off the vino. It was getting to be a problem. She wasn't a kid anymore, and she'd been noticing that the mornings after were getting tougher. It wasn't good for her looks either. Puffiness under the eyes always looked even worse on camera.

Cassie pushed on, reaching St. Armands Circle, now quiet and deserted. She ran

around the loop, passing the carefully deco-
rated display windows, noting Tommy Ba-
hama's and Cafe L'Europe, restaurants that
Leroy had mentioned. As she completed the
circle, she noticed Sebastien Jewelers, connecting it to the man that she had met at Cà
d'Zan the night before.

She headed back over the causeway,
concentrating on the sidewalk in front of her,
forcing herself to keep going. At last, she
was done. A grassy area in front of the marina across the highway from the hotel provided a good place to walk for a while and
cool down. Cassie watched as a few men,
carrying fishing gear, went out to boats bobbing in the choppy water. Still days away
from landfall, Giselle was making her impending fury felt.

Cassie walked out on one of the docks,
stopping at the end to study the cloudy horizon. *You better change your attitude and get
psyched to cover this story, lady. Stop feeling sorry for yourself and get with the program.* Why would Leroy, or anyone else for
that matter, want to work with her? She was
so hangdog all the time. True, she had a lot
on her plate, but many others were far worse
off than she. Cassie had always steered

clear of people with negative attitudes. Now she had become one of those types.

She closed her eyes and promised herself that she was going to change. She was simply going to do the best she could with the things under her control. The rest was out of her hands. Hannah, the lawsuit, her place with KEY, Jim and his relationship with Gillian Cox . . . she couldn't control any of those situations beyond giving her part in them her best effort. Covering a hurricane was a piece of cake compared with dealing with the muddle of her personal and professional life. *Dig in.*

Resolved, Cassie headed back down the dock, stopping by a man lashing heavy rope to a blue sailboat, securing it to the posts of the wooden dock.

"Getting ready for Giselle?"

The man paused and nodded grimly, adjusting his orange cap. "Yeah, and I have a hundred more just like this one to do today."

"Oh, you work here."

"Own the place."

"Really? Well, I'm with KEY News, and we're down here to cover the storm."

"Is that right?" The man didn't sound impressed.

Cassie went on, unperturbed. "We'll probably be doing a story about hurricane preparations. Mind if we come down later and do some shooting? Maybe interview you?"

"Yeah, I suppose that would be all right," answered the man, continuing to wrap the rope. "As long as it doesn't take too much time. I have my hands full here. We lost a lot of boats the last time a big storm blew through, and I can't afford for that to happen again."

"Okay, thanks. I'd appreciate it." Cassie paused, not knowing the man's name. "By the way, I'm Cassie Sheridan."

"Jerry Dean," muttered the man, not looking up from his work.

"Thanks again, Jerry. I'll see you later."

Good. That was a step in the right direction, Cassie thought as she headed back to the hotel. Now she could tell Leroy that she had lined up an interview.

Cassie's constant hotel room companion was the television. She watched *KEY to America* as she peeled off her running clothes and left the set running while she went in to take a shower. With her makeup applied and hair blown dry, she came out just in time to hear the local news report in the affiliate cutaway section of the network broadcast.

"Murder at the Ringling mansion. The body of a prominent Sarasota businessman was found at Cà d'Zan early this morning. Forty-two-year-old Leslie Sebastien, a jeweler with an exclusive shop on St. Armands Circle, was discovered in the mansion's rose garden by a groundskeeper. Sebastien's throat had been slashed. Sebastien had attended the fund-raising concert by the Boys Next Door on the Ringling grounds last night."

That was the man who had complimented her on her ring.

She stared at the video of the rock group that ran on the TV screen. What was *with* this town? Yesterday a hand on the beach. Now a murder. A murder of a man Cassie had met just hours ago.

CHAPTER 25

"The stench coming off that hand was un-freakin'-bearable, and it was so waterlogged that it was tough raising a readable print. The skin was soaked, and the tissue under-neath was really bloated. But I was able to remove the outer layer of skin intact, put it on my own finger, and roll it in the ink. The good news is I got one solid print. I hope it'll be enough, because we don't want to have to go around to every manicure joint in Sara-sota and check who had spiderwebs painted on their nails.

"Look, Danny, I got to go. I got to go look at the body of the guy from the Ringling place. We need this, right? A freakin' hurri-cane's coming. I should be home gettin' my house boarded up."

Deputy Gregg hung up the phone, en-couraged by the prospect that the forensic guys could have an ID on the fingerprint from AFIS by sometime later today. That is, *if* the print was on file with the Automated Fingerprint Identification System.

Danny picked up the framed picture of a smiling Colleen holding a drooling Robbie from its spot on his office desk. He gazed at it with love. He treasured his young family and wanted to keep them safe. Sarasota was where he wanted his son to grow up. Robbie and any other kids he and Colleen were lucky enough to have. He didn't like what the last twenty-four hours had brought to their town.

CHAPTER
26

Thoughts of the pretty pediatric nurse were pushed, for now, from his tortured mind. He had gone to the fund-raiser because it was expected of him, with no idea of how important it would be for him to be there. He believed in destiny. There were no accidents. Eventually the reason for everything that happened in life was revealed. Even Merilee's death, though painful and unplanned, was, ultimately, the way it was supposed to be. And if Leslie Sebastien had to die, that was unfortunate but necessary as well.

Yes, he was *meant* to go to the party last night. Now he knew the ring was out there, and he had to get it back. If the police got their hands on it, the Sebastien hallmark stamped inside the band would lead to the jeweler's sales records, which would, in turn, lead to him.

Sometimes the shameful things he had to cover up overwhelmed him. It had been that way for as long as he could remember. Being caught by his mother with the lingerie he had stolen from his sister and her teenage friends when they spent the night, a neighbor complaining that he was peering into her windows, a teacher finding him hidden in a stall in the girls' bathroom. Those were the things he had been caught at.

There were so many others that no one knew about.

No one knew he was responsible for the attacks on those young women. "Attacks" was what the media called them anyway. He didn't view them that way. He had hoped that those girls secretly enjoyed the time he spent with them, and that they would fall in love with him. Maggie Lynch hadn't killed herself because of their time together. Maggie had killed herself because the media had exposed their most personal shared moments for all the world to see.

He had followed the news coverage, somewhat mollified when Maggie's mother decided to sue KEY News and Cassie Sheridan, the reporter who had bared the intimacy he and Maggie had shared. That wasn't enough for destroying a beautiful, young woman; nevertheless, it had brought some comfort.

But now, Cassie Sheridan was right here in Sarasota.

Destiny.

CHAPTER
27

Banyan trees, their aerial roots dripping with Spanish moss, and statues of cherubs and lions, preening on their pedestals, lined the long driveway leading to Cà d'Zan. The car carrying the KEY News crew drove slowly, observing the hubbub on the Ringling grounds. Yellow police tape cordoned off the perimeter of the rose garden while a news cameraman recorded Sarasota police detectives combing the area around the blood-stained concrete bench under which Leslie Sebastien's body had lain. A couple of hundred yards away, workers broke down the stage where the Boys Next Door had played.

"Too bad this murder is a local story," offered Leroy, as he parked the car next to an SNN News van in the Circus Museum parking lot. "This would be great video."

For their purposes, however, the plan was

only to get some pictures of the mansion's bayside windows being boarded shut in anticipation of the looming storm and conduct a short interview with the Ringling docent. Leroy had made contact with him at the party the night before. *Evening Headlines* wouldn't care about the murder of Leslie Sebastien, and Leroy hadn't even bothered to mention it to New York. From the network news point of view, the murder had no national significance.

As Felix and Leroy unloaded gear from the trunk, Cassie walked across the already steamy parking lot in the direction of the rose garden. A boy, his legs straddling his bicycle, had stationed himself just outside the police tape, craning his sun-bleached head to get a better look at what the police were doing. Cassie recognized him from the local news report. "Hey. You're the one who found the hand on the beach, aren't you?"

The boy looked at her, taking her measure. "Uh-huh."

"That must have been creepy."

"Not really."

Cassie paused to consider the boy's nonchalance. She could play along. "Mmm. Maybe not. Maybe you're used to things like that around here." She nodded in the direction of the bloody bench behind the police tape.

The boy shrugged his thin shoulders beneath his blue Nike T-shirt.

"Hey, Cassie, let's go," Leroy's voice called from the parking lot.

The boy turned to look at the two men, his eyes growing wider when he saw the large black and silver camera. "You with TV?" he asked.

"Yes."

"Doin' a story on the murder?" It was less a question than a statement.

"As a matter of fact, no," said Cassie. "We're here to cover the hurricane."

The boy looked puzzled. "Why would you do a story about a storm that's not even here yet when there's a cool story like this right in front of you?"

"Because I work for the national news. This isn't the sort of story we do. It's kind of complicated, kiddo. But I've got a question for you."

The child waited.

"The news story reported that you were out on the beach with your metal detector when you found the hand, right?"

Vincent nodded.

"Well, I'm wondering what made that detector go off."

"You sound just like my mother," muttered the boy.

"Well?"

"A bottle cap. There was a bottle cap under the seaweed that was on the hand. That's what made the metal detector go off."

"I see," Cassie murmured. She turned to check on Leroy and Felix. "Well, I've got to go, kiddo. Take care."

Vincent couldn't quite tell whether the news lady believed him, but he tagged along behind her, stopping to prop his bike against a banyan tree. She sure was pretty, like all those ladies on TV were. Not like his mother, who looked so tired and messy sometimes.

He followed the news crew around to the back of Cà d'Zan, where Anthony was waiting on the terrace. Carpenters on ladders and scaffolding were nailing sheets of plywood over the stained glass windows. Felix busied himself getting pans and push-ins of the activity.

"I see you've met Vincent," said Anthony, nodding in the boy's direction. The child had stopped at the edge of the terrace, far enough away that he was out of earshot. "He's mad at me because I had to cancel on him again this morning for a lesson on clown makeup. You should probably interview him, he's around here so much. He knows everything."

"Does his mother know he's out here, hanging around a murder scene?"

"I doubt it. I get the impression Vincent is pretty much on his own when he leaves home in the morning."

If my kid had found a human hand on the beach, I'd damn well keep him with me the next day, thought Cassie. But then she realized that she shouldn't make judgments without knowing the situation better.

"You all set?" Cassie called to Felix.

The cameraman gave the thumbs-up sign.

"First of all, would you please state your name and spell it?" Cassie was glad that Felix had miked this interviewee. It was awkward enough looking down at him. She was glad she didn't have to keep holding a microphone down to him.

"Anthony Dozier. D-O-Z-I-E-R."

"And your position?"

"I'm a Ringling docent."

"How long have you been a docent here?"

"Twelve years. Since I left the circus."

"Oh? What did you do in the circus?"

"I was a clown."

Images of a little greasepainted man running around the circus ring passed through Cassie's mind. If she let it, the thought could make her feel sad. *Move on.* But, involuntarily, she envisioned the FBI sketch of Maggie Lynch's attacker.

"Okay, Mr. Dozier. Could you tell me what you are doing to get ready for Giselle?" she asked.

"Well, as you can see, we are boarding up the place as best we can. The mansion here recently underwent a major restoration, and we don't want all that work and money to blow away."

Cassie looked out at the green bay water. "You're all in a pretty precarious spot here, aren't you, Mr. Dozier? Right on the water like this."

"That comes with the territory. Today, just as when John Ringling built this place back in the nineteen twenties, waterfront is prime real estate. Most people who can afford to buy or build on the water are willing to take the risk of an occasional storm."

What else could she ask? This would be just a small part of the story on the storm preps they would offer the *Evening Headlines* tonight. They could use the docent's sound bite about people willing to risk a storm for the pleasure of living on the water or they could use the one about waiting to see how bad the forecast got. Either way, they had enough of Anthony Dozier.

Cassie wished she hadn't walked around to the front of the mansion ahead of Leroy and Felix when she saw Sarge Tucker talking to one of the stagehands breaking down the Boys Next Door stage set. The promoter spotted her before she could turn back.

As he approached, Cassie noticed that his face didn't have the revved-up glow of the evening before. "Finished talking to the midget?" Sarge sneered.

Cassie didn't respond to the slur.

"I got up to watch the KEY morning show at that godforsaken hour, but I didn't see a damn thing about the boys," Sarge declared.

Dammit! Leroy should be taking the heat

for this, not her. It had been his bright idea. "I'm sorry, Mr. Tucker. But that's how it goes sometimes. We can never promise that something is going to make air."

Sarge wasn't buying it. "I think I was duped. That's what I think. You never intended to have the boys on."

He was right, and Cassie didn't feel like making any other excuses for Leroy's deception. Still, it was all part of the game. Promoters were forever inviting the media to events in the hopes that their clients, big and small, would get television exposure. Sometimes they got it, sometimes they didn't. There were no guarantees. Sarge Tucker surely knew that.

"All I can say is I'm sorry, Mr. Tucker."

There was a momentary awkward silence, and Cassie began to continue toward the crew car. But Sarge called after her. "That's pretty mean business over there, isn't it?" He thrust his chin in the direction of the cordoned-off rose garden.

"Yes, it is. Did you know the man who was murdered?"

Sarge fingered one of the gold chains around his neck. "Not well. But I did go in his shop from time to time. It's sure a shame he was killed, but it made certain that our concert was on the front page of the newspaper and on local TV this morning. You know what they say," said Sarge with an arch wink. "Bad publicity is better than no publicity."

"I've heard it, but I really don't agree with it."

What a huckster. Cassie walked away in disgust.

The boy pedaled along beside her. "You didn't like that guy, did you?"

"What makes you say that?"

"I could just tell by the way you talked to him."

"You shouldn't be eavesdropping on other people's conversations, Vincent."

The child was not rebuffed. "I learn a lot of good stuff that way."

They reached the parking lot. Cassie opened the car door to let out the hot air.

"I didn't like him either," Vincent offered.

"Oh you didn't, huh? Why not?"

"He looked like a girl with all those gold necklaces. And I didn't like the way he talked about Anthony." Vincent looked away for a moment. "And I didn't like the way he talked to you."

Cassie smiled. "Thank you, kind sir, but you don't have to worry about me." She looked directly into the youngster's eyes. "I'm going to let you in on a little secret, Vincent, a secret that it took me years to figure out. It's usually a good idea to trust your instincts."

Cassie and Leroy sat in the air-conditioned Jeep as Felix slammed the door on the trunk full of gear. Two men approached, one in a summer sports jacket and tie, the other in a turquoise SNN T-shirt. Cassie opened her window.

"Hi, again. Remember me? I'm Tony Whitcomb from Suncoast News Network."

Cassie shook the clammy hand stuck through the window. "Right. We met last night."

"Yeah, I just wanted to say hello again and tell you how much I admire your work."

"Thanks."

"I watch KEY all the time. I dream of working at the network level someday."

Poor guy. Cassie managed a polite smile.

"But I know you need connections to get there," Tony continued. "I have some stories

I'm really proud of, but I need the right people to see them."

"Do you have an agent?"

Tony shook his head. "No. I suppose I should get one, huh?"

"It might help."

"Yeah, I guess I'll have to look into that." The prospect of paying someone a percentage of his earnings didn't appeal to him. "Any chance I could send you my tape and you pass it on to the powers that be at KEY?"

Well, the guy certainly had chutzpah. What the heck? It wouldn't cost her anything to send it on to New York. "Sure, I guess I could do that. No promises though."

"Great, Cassie. Thanks a lot. I'll get that tape to you right away. Where should I send it?"

She ripped a sheet from her notepad and wrote down the Miami Bureau address.

As they drove away from the Ringling grounds, Leroy remarked, "They all think the network is the promised land."

"They should only know," said Felix. "Did you get a load of the shooter's camera? It was better than mine."

CHAPTER
28

By calling in sick right after the murder scene pictures, Brian would reap the benefits for a double payday. SNN would still pay him for a day's work while he'd earn a nice fat check from Webb for working on *Velvet Nights.* But when he called the station to say he wasn't coming in, the assignment editor informed him that the sheriff's department had come and taken the video Brian had shot at Cà d'Zan the night before. They wanted to see if there was anything on the tape that would help in the investigation of Leslie Sebastien's murder.

Brian cursed himself for not dubbing off the tape after the late news the night before. Now the cops had the only copy. Webb wasn't going to like that.

The cameraman tried to recall what was

on the tape. Varied shots of the guests, many taken from the back. Most, though, were of Gloria, with many focused on the cleavage above her gold lamé gown. That would look bad.

CHAPTER
29

Thank the good Lord, Charles was with her! Etta was so nervous she couldn't think straight, and she was relieved that she had her husband to deal with the nurse at the reception desk about all the health insurance business.

Charles took the seat next to hers in the waiting area, and Etta grabbed hold of his hand.

"Will you look at that," said Charles, pointing to a poster on the wall and trying to distract her. "Contact lenses that change the color of your eyes."

Etta moved her head up and down automatically but said nothing, unable to concentrate on what Charles was saying.

The door at the side of the waiting room opened. "Mrs. Chambers?" called another nurse.

"Yes. I'm here," Etta answered in a weak voice.

"You can come in now."

Giving one last squeeze to Charles's hand, Etta rose to her feet and followed the nurse.

"Which eye are you having done today, Mrs. Chambers?" asked the nurse, looking at her clipboard.

"My left." Dr. Lewis had assured Etta that it would be safe to do both eyes at once, but she didn't want to take the chance. What if something went wrong? No, she'd do one eye first and then, after seeing how it worked out, come back in a couple of months and have the other one done.

The nurse placed a green adhesive-backed dot above Etta's left eye. "Would you put your head back, please, Mrs. Chambers?" The nurse squeezed four drops into Etta's eye. "These will cleanse and numb your eye."

At intervals of several minutes, the nurse repeated the procedure with the drops a few more times. Then she helped Etta put a robe on over her clothes, covered her shoes with blue paper booties, and fitted an elasticized cap over her silver hair. Etta sat in a reclining chair and waited while the anesthesiologist inserted an IV needle in the back of her hand.

"This is to relax you, Mrs. Chambers."

"Um-hmm." She could barely get out the response.

Five minutes later she was escorted into the operating room and laid down on the table. Her eye was taped open and her face covered with gauze, leaving just her left eye exposed for surgery. She heard the door open and Dr. Lewis's voice as he entered the room. "Okay, Etta. Here we go." The lamp he wore on his forehead beamed into her eye, a bright, intense light.

The Valium must be working. She suddenly felt like talking. "Did you have a nice time at the party last night, Dr. Lewis?" she asked.

"It was okay. Though I'm not exactly a big Boys Next Door fan. Do you feel anything, Etta?"

"No."

"Ready to insert the lens. You may feel tugging or pressure as I insert the lens, Etta."

But Etta felt nothing as the new lens was slid in through the slit on the side of her eyeball.

"That was terrible, wasn't it, Dr. Lewis, about that poor man they found murdered? I keep thinking I had only just checked his name off on the guest list when he arrived. He never suspected that last night's party would be his last."

"Yes. I saw it on the news this morning. It's a terrible thing."

"My husband bought me a bracelet from Leslie Sebastien's jewelry store for our anniversary just last month," Etta rambled on from beneath the surgical cloth. "And did I tell you? Yesterday morning, I was on the beach when that little boy found the hand."

"No. I don't think you mentioned that," said Dr. Lewis.

"It still gives me shivers. I feel sorry for that poor woman, whoever she was."

"How do you know it was a woman? I didn't hear that it was a woman's hand on the news."

"Well, I guess it could have been a man's, if he wore red nail polish with a spiderweb stenciled on top."

He hung his white lab coat in the closet. After his morning surgeries and early afternoon office hours, Harry Lewis was eager to leave work, stop home to change, and get down to the marina. The conversation with the old Chambers gal had him worried.

He tried to see Merilee as little as possible. One of the city's leading doctors didn't really want to be seen in the company of a porno queen.

It had started innocently enough. He'd actually met her at the Publix of all places, walking down the frozen-food aisle. She had been so scrubbed and clean-looking, her jet black hair swept back from her face in a neat ponytail, no makeup on her high cheekbones. He'd watched her as she put ice cream in her shopping cart. He still remembered. Chocolate chip mint.

He had lingered, longer than he had to, and then, as unobtrusively as he could, he followed her around the supermarket until she went to the checkout line. He took his place in the line behind her, watching as she pulled a magazine from the rack and browsed through it while she waited her turn.

It was while she unloaded her groceries from the cart onto the conveyor belt that he had noticed her nails. Long and bright red.

She must have felt him staring at her, because she looked his way and smiled. He'd smiled back and started the conversation.

They'd had several dinners together before she told him what she actually did for a living. What the hospital board of directors could do with that!

Harry had tried to break it off, but he couldn't help himself. He could go for a few weeks, but then, hating himself, he'd call Merilee again.

In between times, he had her videos to keep him warm.

CHAPTER
30

The morning's shoot was not going well. Webb was not pleased with his actors' gyrations beneath the papier-mâché facsimiles of the babies Romulus and Remus, and their wolf mother. After the third take, Webb yelled at the actors beneath the twisted sheets. "Nobody's going to pay a dime to see *Velvet Nights in Venice* if you don't try to look like you're enjoying yourself, Gloria. And, Van, the sneer on your face makes the wolf's snout look friendly. Lighten up for God's sake. This is a fantasy piece, not a horror flick."

Brian waited until they broke for lunch before giving Webb the bad news. As the cast and crew lined up at the catered buffet, he pulled the producer to the side of the studio.

"What do you mean, the police have the tape?" Webb demanded, his face growing florid.

"I'm sorry, boss, I really am. But there's nothing I could do about it."

"You should have made a dub."

"Yeah, I know I should've. But I was tired and I just wanted to get home."

"That's just great. Now you've had your damned beauty sleep, but I don't have the material for my opening!" Webb's face was red beneath his tan.

Brian cast around for a silver lining. "Look, Webb, the station is going to be using the material that aired last night over and over any time they do a story on the murder. The cops are going to be poring over the out-takes with a magnifying glass. People are going to become familiar with that tape and what's on it. Maybe it's better this way. Maybe you don't want to use the video after all."

The cameraman might well have a point, but Webb didn't feel like acknowledging it. "Maybe, schmaybe," he snarled. "Maybe I like to have the option of deciding what and what not to include in my work. Now, thanks to you, I don't have any choice."

Wrapped in her purple silk bathrobe, Gloria sat alone in the dressing room, picking at her macaroni salad and seething. Her litany of grievances played over and over in her mind. It was all too evident that Van hadn't brushed his teeth this morning, and her chapped skin testified to the fact that he hadn't bothered to shave. He had been rough as he turned her body and careful to make sure that it was his best attributes that were shown to the camera, not giving a hoot about how she looked or if he was blocking her. It just wasn't professional.

At first Gloria had tried to make good on her mental vow to show Van a great time in appreciation for his support over her taking Merilee's role. But now she was getting the idea that it wasn't that Van wanted to work with her. Rather, it was that he *didn't* want to work with Merilee. Though Gloria didn't like admitting it to herself, Merilee, by her sheer star power, did dominate every scene she was in. She was magnetic.

The dressing room door opened before Gloria had a chance to respond to the brief knock. She wrapped the robe closer around herself as Van entered. "Truce?" he offered.

Gloria gazed into her paper plate and was silent.

"Come on, baby." Van walked over to the

dressing table and picked up a makeup brush. Inspecting himself in the mirror, he expertly powdered under his dark eyes, camouflaging the puffy circles. "We both have a lot riding on this one, Gloria. Let's go back out there and show 'em we got what it takes."

Gloria observed him as he continued working on his face. The glaring makeup bulbs highlighted the wrinkles around Van's eyes and mouth. Merilee had been right when she complained that she deserved a younger costar. Van was getting too old for this business, and he undoubtedly knew it. He could pump all the iron he wanted, even go for a face-lift, but the camera would forgive only so much.

Feeling her eyes on him, Van turned to face Gloria. "What are you thinking about?" It sounded more like an accusation than a question.

"Nothing," she said guiltily.

"I can tell. You are thinking about something." His tone grew more menacing.

"No, I'm not."

"You know what I think, Gloria? He moved toward her, taking hold of her silk-clad arm. "I think that you shouldn't underestimate me.

I think that you should know who's in charge here." His grip grew tighter.

Gloria tried to laugh him off. "Come on, Van. Stop clowning around. We're too old for this." She tried to twist her arm away.

At that, he struck her.

Gloria raised her free arm to shield her face. "Van, stop! Please, stop! Not my face!" she whimpered.

His open hand froze in midair as he remembered that they had to be back out on the set in a few minutes. His other fist released her arm.

"Stop crying," he hissed. "Wash your face and put on some fresh makeup. But remember, I call the shots, Gloria. Understand? You damned well better get out there and follow my lead this afternoon. This is my movie."

"I'm going to tell Webb," Gloria threatened, sobbing.

Van stopped at the door. "You do that, and maybe you'll go missing, too."

CHAPTER 31

Leroy simply went into the Publix at Bee Ridge Road, found the store manager, and asked if they could come in and shoot customers stocking up on supplies. With permission granted, Felix shot in the aisles that held canned goods, bottled water, and batteries. Cassie interviewed people as they came out of the supermarket, getting their takes on the upcoming storm.

"They say Sarasota hasn't been hit by a major hurricane in over forty years. I figure it's only a matter of time before our luck runs out," said a mother with a young child sitting in her shopping cart.

"I just got an evacuation zone map because I have no idea where I'm supposed to go," responded another woman in a business suit.

"I was in the Keys when Hurricane Donna

slammed in, back in 1960," said a retiree. "Let me tell you, it wasn't pretty."

After a few more short interviews, Cassie's rumbling stomach told her it was time for lunch. She and Felix went back to the car, where Leroy was on his cell phone with New York. "They aren't sure if they're going to use us tonight or not," he said, snapping the phone closed. All three knew that meant they would have to proceed as if they were going to make air anyway. "Let's go out to a beach and get some stuff there." He checked his map. "The closest beach is Siesta."

"Well, I'm starving," chimed Felix to Cassie's relief. "Let's stop and get something to eat."

"We'll find someplace on the way," said the producer.

They took Siesta Drive over the North Bridge and followed the curve that led them to Ocean Boulevard. They parked in front of the first place they found to eat. An open-air joint on the left-hand side of the road. The Old Salty Dog.

Most of the weathered picnic tables were empty. Cassie hoped that was not an indication of how the food was going to be. She ordered the English fish-and-chips, while Leroy and Felix ordered what the menu proclaimed to be the specialty of the house, Famous Salty Dogs—hot dogs dipped in beer batter and deep-fried.

"This may be a heart attack waiting to happen, but it's the best damn thing I've eaten in a while," said Leroy, munching away on the first of his two dogs.

Cassie supposed the deep-fried fillet of cod and the mound of golden french fries that filled her basket weren't much healthier, but she didn't care. It was delicious.

"Want a refill on that Diet Coke?" asked the blond waitress.

"Yes. Thanks," answered Cassie. "The food is terrific." She glanced at the empty tables around them. "I don't understand why there aren't more people here."

"It's our slow season," said the waitress. "That, and I think people must be getting ready for the storm."

A man wearing an apron came out from the kitchen. "Hey, Wendy, your son is on the phone."

"Excuse me," said the waitress. Cassie noticed the varicose vein on the back of the

woman's leg as she walked away. It was a tough way to make a living.

Vincent was angry as he hung up the phone. That was what he got for asking permission. A big, fat no. He was stuck inside the house on one of his last free afternoons because his mother had been called to work and he had to baby-sit for Mark again. It wasn't fair.

Vincent looked at the clock on the kitchen wall. It would be another two hours before his mother got home. He didn't want to wait that long. "Come on, Mark," he said, making up his mind. They could go to the beach and find Gideon and be back before their mother returned. If Mark kept his mouth shut, their mother would never be the wiser.

CHAPTER
32

Though he could ill afford the time away from the marina, Jerry drove home at lunchtime. His muscles were aching and he craved a hot shower. He had lots more to do with the boats, but he had to take care of himself or he wouldn't make it through.

He came out of the bathroom with a towel tied around his waist and held out a tube of Ben-Gay. "Put this on for me, will ya, Karen?"

His sister smoothed the ointment over Jerry's back and shoulders. The stinging warmth penetrated his sore body. "Oh man, that feels good."

"You're getting quite a little gut there, Jerry boy," Karen teased.

"That's none of your business," he growled, sucking in his stomach.

"Touchy, touchy." She laughed.

Jerry grabbed the tube away from her and

went to get dressed. When he came out of his room, a roast beef sandwich and side of potato salad were waiting for him on the kitchen table. He wolfed his lunch down as Karen watched. "Stop staring at me, will you?"

"I don't know what the hell's the matter with you today, Jerry, but don't take your problems out on me."

"There's a little thing like a hurricane coming, Karen, or haven't you heard?"

"Yeah, obnoxious one, I've heard. As a matter of fact, you'll be glad to know I'm getting out of here till things blow over. I'm leaving this afternoon to go up to see Mom."

Good riddance. He wanted the place to himself.

He wished he had never let her move in after her divorce. It was supposed to be a temporary thing, just until she got on her feet again. But six months later she still had no job and spent her days watching talk shows and soap operas. Jerry hoped Karen would be away for a good, long time. She was cramping his style.

CHAPTER
33

Those parasailors were pushing the envelope, thought Deputy Gregg as he scanned the sky over the Gulf, watching their multicolored parachute sails quivering in the increasing winds. But, then again, this was the sort of weather that thrill seekers loved.

He dismounted his ATV after his midday patrol, wondering when the call would be made to issue a small-craft warning and close the beach. It was already fairly deserted, save for the walkers and runners. The graying skies made sunbathing useless.

As he entered his office at the pavilion, the phone was ringing. "Danny, it's Bill in Forensics. I thought you'd want to know. We got a match on that print. AFIS had it on file from an old shoplifting charge."

"What's the name?" asked Danny.

"Merilee Quiñones. We've got an address on her. And, get this, Danny. One of the guys recognized her name. She stars in porno flicks!"

CHAPTER
34

Sarge was putting this last concert of the tour on autopilot. His head was pounding, and there was no way he was driving up to Tampa tonight. All was in place. The free press passes had been sent to the newspapers, radio stations, and local television stations. He didn't have to be there. His assistant could cover things. The promoter was relieved that the tour was finally over. Life on the road wasn't what it was cracked up to be. It was a stressful grind.

When Sarge had signed on with the Boys Next Door, it had been fun to watch them become more and more popular, fun to be part of the team effort to make the group the sensation they now were. The sweetest pleasure and greatest satisfaction was that Sarge had brought them the song that became their biggest hit. "Brown-Eyed Baby" had gone platinum. Sarge's name was on the CD label as songwriter, and the royalty checks had made him a wealthy man. He expected "Nobody Knows" to bring him even more good fortune.

Sarge took a bottle of ibuprofen from the medicine cabinet and swallowed three tablets as the doorbell rang. He considered not answering, but the buzzing was persistent.

Two men in sports jackets, holding unfolded police credentials, stood outside. Sarge was unaware that they had just come from searching the condominium next door. "We're detectives with the Sarasota Sheriff's Department. We'd like to ask you a few questions."

Sarge looked closely at the credentials and waved the men inside, offering them a seat. One detective took notes, writing down Sarge's name on a spiral pad, while the other asked the questions.

"Mr. Tucker, do you know your neighbor, Merilee Quiñones?"

"Of course I know her. She lives next door, doesn't she?" Sarge was already aggravated with these guys.

"Do you know her well?"

"I wouldn't say 'well.' She only moved in here about a year ago. I travel a lot, so I'm not around that much."

"What do you do for a living, Mr. Tucker?"

"I'm in the music business." Sarge indicated the framed gold record that hung over the sofa. "I promote the Boys Next Door."

The detective rose from his chair and walked across the room to inspect the plaque. "Mmm. 'Brown-Eyed Baby.' That your song? My daughter dances around to that all the time."

"Glad to hear it."

The detective squinted to read the small black print on the gold-plated disc. "It says here you wrote the song. I thought you said you promoted the band."

"That's right. But I play around with music a little bit, too."

"That's pretty impressive."

"I read in the newspaper this morning that

your band played a brand-new song at Ring-ling last night."

"Yes. 'Nobody Knows.' I wrote that, too."

The detective didn't comment as he went back to his chair. "When was the last time you saw Miss Quiñones?"

Sarge thought fast. How should he respond? Someone could have seen them talking. "It must have been last week sometime," he answered, trying to appear nonchalant as he considered his next words. "Yes, as a matter of fact, it was a week ago today. I had to come back into town to take care of some business, and I saw Merilee in the driveway."

"What did you talk about?"

"Nothing special, as I recall," Sarge lied. "She was excited about the band coming to Sarasota for a concert."

"So you must have been at the concert at Cà d'Zan last night?" the detective led, glancing at his partner.

"Yes, I was." Sarge shifted uncomfortably on the sofa, anticipating what was coming.

"I suppose you are aware that there was a murder after the concert last night."

Sarge nodded.

"Did you know the man who was murdered? Leslie Sebastien?"

"Vaguely. I patronized his jewelry store occasionally."

"That's quite a coincidence, Mr. Tucker. You know Mr. Sebastien *and* Miss Quiñones?"

"I don't catch your drift."

"Well, we know Mr. Sebastien was murdered and we have reason to believe that Miss Quiñones was. You knew them both."

The detectives got into their car.

"What do you think?" asked one.

The other shrugged. "I don't know. He looked genuinely surprised when you said the woman was dead."

"He could be just a good actor. We already know he was lying about one thing."

"You mean about not really knowing the porno queen?"

"Mmm-hmm. That file on her desk was thick with clippings about the success of the Boys Next Door, and that letter from the attorney leaves no doubt that she was going to sue the pants off our friend Mr. Tucker."

The car pulled down the driveway from the condominium complex.

"I don't know, Jack," said the driver. "Do you really think she could have written that new song?"

"Whether she did or she didn't, you can bet the band's promoter, the same guy that takes credit for writing the song himself, wouldn't want the hassle and expense of a lawsuit. Not to mention all that bad publicity."

CHAPTER
35

Vincent so wanted to know how much Gideon had gotten for the ring last night, but his friend was not at his post on the pier. So that the forbidden trek to the beach wouldn't be a total loss, Vincent pulled Mark along the shoreline and looked for sharks' teeth.

"Sharks are always losing their teeth and growing new ones . . . thousands of them!" He recited for his little brother the facts that Gideon had taught him. "Some of these teeth we're finding are prehistoric, Mark, because sharks have lived around here for millions of years. The teeth drop to the bottom of the sea, and then they wash up on the shore because of the waves and the tides."

Mark squatted down to inspect the wet sand. "Here's one!" the boy proclaimed, holding a small, smooth, black triangle up for Vincent to see.

Vincent studied the tooth. "That's cool. But what's really sweet is finding a white one, because that's from a *living* shark. I have hundreds of these black ones, and gray ones and brown ones. Those are the old ones. But I only have two white ones. Those are the best."

Mark listened to his brother with the wide-eyed wonder that the younger has for an older sibling. They continued sifting through the sand until, inevitably, Mark began to cough. Vincent wanted to smack him. He was always messing up everything.

"Come on," he said grudgingly, "we better go back before Mom gets home. And you better not tell her we came out here or I'll kill you."

"I won't tell, Vincent. I promise."

The brothers began to trudge through the sand. Vincent glanced down the beach and noticed with excitement the television people he had seen up at Ringling this morning. The camera guy was taking pictures of that Cassie lady standing with her back to the Gulf, talking into her microphone. Vincent pulled Mark's arm and made him run in time to hear Cassie record her stand-up.

"Late this afternoon, a small-craft advisory was posted along the Gulf coast, officials warning small boats not to venture into the open sea. Sarasota is now on an official hurricane watch, which means forecasters think Giselle, at least until Thursday morning, poses a threat to coastal areas here. A hurricane watch means that hurricane conditions are a real possibility. It *does not* mean a storm is about to strike. Cassie Sheridan, KEY News, Siesta Key, Florida."

As the reporter unclipped her microphone, she looked over and recognized Vincent. "You again, huh? You get around, don't you?"

"So do you."

"I suppose you're right." Cassie smiled with amusement. "Who's this?"

"It's only my little brother."

"Does your little brother have a name?"

"Mark."

"Hello, Mark." Cassie bent forward to

shake the child's hand. The boy began to cough.

"Aww. He's always doing that." Vincent was impatient. "He has cystic fibrosis."

"I see," said Cassie softly. "That must be hard for *both* of you."

Vincent looked at her skeptically. Did she really understand? Nobody ever seemed to. They were always feeling sorry for Mark but never paid any attention to how hard it was for *him*. Squirming, Vincent changed the subject. "Hey, you want to interview me?"

"Haven't you been on television enough lately?"

"Yeah, that's why I'd be good to talk to. I know what I'm doing."

Cassie winked at Felix. "Okay, why not?" She clipped her microphone to Vincent's T-shirt.

"Tell me what you think about a hurricane coming."

"I think it's really neat. I've never been in a hurricane before."

"You're not afraid?"

"Of course not."

"Do you know what you'll do if a hurricane comes?"

Vincent stopped to consider the question.

"I guess I'll stay inside and watch out the window."

"They are talking about evacuations. Do you know what that means?"

"Of course I do. I'm not stupid."

"Sorry. Well, do you know where your nearest hurricane shelter is?"

Vincent bit at the corner of his mouth. His younger brother was beginning to look frightened. Cassie had the feeling she should stop with the questions. "I'm sure your mother knows where to go," she said hastily. "I think we have enough now, Vincent."

"Will I be on television again tonight?" The hope on his freckled face was visible.

"I'm not sure. It depends if the people who run our news show in New York decide that this story is important enough for all the people around the United States to see."

Fearing that he hadn't come across as well as he'd hoped to, Vincent wanted to redeem himself in the reporter's eyes. "Hey, want to see where I found the hand yesterday? It's right up there." He pointed to the seawall.

While Felix packed up the camera gear,

Cassie allowed herself to be dragged to the scene of the washed-up hand.

"Weren't you scared?" she asked, looking at the spot in the sand that Vincent indicated.

"No. Man, I wasn't scared. When I saw that ring, I was excited!" The proud expression on his face changed the moment he realized what he had let slip.

"A ring, huh? So that's what made the detector go off."

Vincent grabbed Mark's hand. "We gotta go. My mother will be mad if we're not back when she gets home."

CHAPTER
36

He left the car motor running because the thick humidity made air-conditioning a must. From the curbside vantage point across the street from Sebastien Jewelers, he watched and waited, listening to the radio. "Nobody Knows" played. It sure was catchy. He tapped his palm against the steering wheel. The music from the rock station was inter- rupted by a weather report. Giselle was gathering speed.

He caressed the scraggly beard he had glued on his chin as he watched a few well- heeled shoppers stroll by, carrying their pur- chases in brightly colored bags. Some customers loitered on the sidewalk in front of the closed jewelry store, pointing and whis- pering among themselves and shaking their heads before moving along.

A glance into the rearview mirror revealed that some of the powder he had combed through his hair had sprinkled onto his shoulder. He brushed it away.

A few minutes past five o'clock, he watched the old man with the shock of white hair pull at Sebastien's door. When it didn't budge, the codger pressed his cupped hands against the plate glass, his eyes peer- ing into the dimness within.

A patrolman making his rounds about St. Armands Circle stopped to talk to the old guy, probably explaining why the jewelry store hadn't opened that day. The geezer pulled at the ends of his white mustache as he listened. The old man turned, walked to his tired automobile, and maneuvered it out of its parking space.

Music blared in the shiny late-model car, with windows rolled up tight against the thick summer air, that followed the old Plymouth back over the causeway.

CHAPTER
37

Leslie Sebastien's throat had been slit, thought Gideon, like the gullet of one of the fish from the Gulf. Maybe it was just a coincidence that the jeweler had been murdered hours after Gideon had talked to him about the ring, but Gideon didn't like the feeling he had about the whole deal. He was going to talk to Vincent and convince the boy that the ring had to be turned over to the cops. In the meantime, he had to find a safe place to stash it.

Gideon pulled his old Plymouth into the sandy driveway and switched off the ignition. He got out of the car and walked to the back porch of his small, weather-beaten ranch, the screen door creaking as he opened it.

His tacklebox lay on the stone floor. A nice little safety deposit box.

Gideon tucked the ring beneath his favorite lures but left the tackle case where it lay. If he brought it inside, it would look out of place, defeating the whole idea of hiding in plain sight.

The door from the kitchen to the back porch opened. Vincent stood with an excited expression on his face. "I've been looking for you all day. Did you get it, Gideon? Did you get the money for the ring?"

"I see you let yourself in again," Gideon observed. "No, boy, I didn't get the money."

"Why not?"

The ashen look on the fisherman's face told the boy something was wrong.

"I didn't get the money because the man who owned the jewelry store wasn't there to buy the ring from me."

"Oh," said Vincent, momentarily crestfallen. "Well, you can go back tomorrow, right?"

"No, Vincent, I won't be going back tomorrow."

"Why not?"

"Because the man who owns the store is dead. He was killed last night up at some party at the Ringling estate."

Vincent quickly put together the crime scene excitement he had witnessed that morning and the report he had seen on the news while he was waiting for Gideon to come home. The guy who had been murdered was the guy who owned the jewelry store Gideon was using as a fence for the ruby ring! For the moment, the anticipation of the windfall from the ring was forgotten, replaced with the nervous thrill of putting two and two together in a real murder case.

"Yeah! I wanted to find you today and tell you, Gideon. I wanted to tell you about the murder up at Ringling. I saw the cops up there this morning, investigating. I even saw the blood on the ground!"

"You did, did you?"

Vincent's head bobbed, his mind running ahead. It was too bad the jewelry guy was killed, but there were other jewelers who would want to buy the ring.

Gideon sat down at the kitchen table and beckoned Vincent to take the wooden chair across from him. "Listen, son, I should have told you this sooner. I think we have to turn the ring over to the police."

The boy's face fell. "No way."

"Yes," the old man said firmly. "You have to give it to the cops, Vincent. It could help them figure out who that hand belongs to."

"But they already know who it belongs to," Vincent announced triumphantly. "I saw it on the news just now. It was some lady's hand who lived right here in Sarasota."

"Since when do you watch the news so much?" Gideon asked skeptically.

"Since yesterday. I wanted to see if they used my picture again. And they did, Gideon. They showed me again. And they had a picture of the lady. So you see? The police don't need the ring. They already know whose hand it was."

Gideon got up from the table and opened the refrigerator, considering what Vincent had told him as he poured himself a glass of iced tea from a plastic pitcher. "Want one?" he offered.

The boy's face scrunched up. "Yuck. Besides, I got to get home. I have to watch my brother and my mom's going to kill me. I'm late."

Vincent wiggled uncomfortably in his chair. He knew he wouldn't be able to wait until he got home. "I have to hit the can before I go."

He had parked the car a couple of doors down from the driveway that the Plymouth had pulled into and waited a few minutes while he considered how to go about what he needed to do. The old coot looked strong for someone his age, but he could definitely take him on. He patted the bulge in his pants pocket.

It was still daylight, but he didn't think he had to wait until dark. Though the surrounding houses were relatively close together, there was lots of overgrown vegetation between them. He got out of the car and walked toward the house, turning with confidence into the driveway. If anyone was watching, it would only arouse suspicion if he looked like he was skulking.

A bike was propped against the side of the ranch, but he didn't think anything of it. Through the screen door, he could see the old man sitting at the table with his back to the porch.

*   *   *

What excuse was he going to give his mother this time? Vincent wondered as he sat in the bathroom. He dreaded going home. He didn't want to face his mother's wrath and he didn't want to spend another night with Mark and that awful pounding treatment. It wasn't fair. Mom had already worked the lunch shift, and now she had to cover the evening shift, too. So he got stuck.

Resigned to facing his destiny, Vincent pulled at the roll of toilet paper. He was reaching for the toilet handle when he heard voices from the other side of the closed door.

"Who are you? And what the hell do you want?" Gideon demanded, deliberately raising his voice, hoping that Vincent would hear him, praying the boy wouldn't come out of the bathroom.

"Where is it? I want that ring."

"I don't know what you're talking about."

"Cut the crap, old man. You have the ring and I want it. Now."

Gideon stared at the cold steel blade that was pointed in his direction. He should turn over the ring. It wasn't worth getting killed for. He wanted to get this guy out of the house before Vincent came back. Gideon rose from his chair, cringing as he thought he heard the bathroom door open.

The intruder heard it, too.

In the split second that the intruder turned to look in the direction of the noise, Gideon lunged.

Vincent slammed and locked the bathroom door.

His heart pounding against his chest wall, he climbed into the bathtub and yanked desperately at the small window. The frame was stuck, swollen by the humidity.

Violent banging reverberated from the other side of the bathroom door.

With all his might, Vincent pushed at the window. It gave slightly.

Another push, and then another, as the pounding on the door grew louder.

Finally, the door gave, crashing into the tiny bathroom.

The intruder pulled back the plastic shower curtain.

The window was open. But only enough for a child or a midget to slip through.

CHAPTER
38

In her room at the hotel, Cassie caught the SNN evening broadcast. *Quite a hopping city, Sarasota,* she thought as she watched the opening story about the murder of the jeweler Leslie Sebastien.

"And we have a follow-up on the story we reported about the hand that was found on Siesta Beach yesterday," continued the local anchorman. "Sheriff's Department officials say that a fingerprint identifies the hand as that of twenty-five-year-old Merilee Quiñones of Sarasota. There are reports that Ms. Quiñones was a performer in adult entertainment videos. Police are continuing their investigation."

Cassie's mind instantly snapped back to the overheard conversation at the Ringling party. Merilee was not a common name. Was it possible that the missing Merilee those three at the bar were talking about last night, the Merilee who was claimed to have written the song being played by one of the biggest boy bands in the country, was the same woman whose hand had washed up on the beach? Now this was a story New York might be interested in. The porno angle was also intriguing. It was worth checking out. And what, if anything, did Merilee Quiñones and the murdered jeweler have to do with each other?

She listened to the rest of the local news, paying special attention to the weather report, followed by the half-hour network broadcast, watching with frustration as the closing credits of the *KEY Evening Headlines* finally rolled.

A full day of shooting and all that aired on the program was twenty seconds of video showing shoppers pulling bottled water and supplies off the grocery store shelves. The anchorwoman, Eliza Blake, voiced over the footage, explaining to the audience only that Floridians in the western part of the state were preparing for Giselle. *What a waste of a day's work.*

She dialed her home in Virginia and got Jim's voice on the answering machine.

"Hi, it's me. Just checking in to see how

you are up there. Love and miss you, Hannah." With a melancholy feeling, she hung up the phone. Where were they? Out for a little dinner with Mrs. Cox?

Cassie pulled back the drapes from the windowed wall and looked over to the marina. There were at least two hours until the sun set, yet the sky was darkening ominously over the Gulf. The leaves of the palm trees rustled in the stiffening breeze. Boats were rocking in the water.

Leroy had blown off her suggestion to shoot at the marina today, but tomorrow she was going to insist they go and interview Jerry Dean and any owners that were over there worrying about their boats. She had to get more assertive and, yes, demanding with Leroy. She was the correspondent, after all. It was her face and name that went on the product, not his. But Cassie had felt so beaten down over these past months that she hadn't had the energy or the inclination to set him straight. In fact, she had been relieved to let him call the shots. That couldn't go on.

Resolved, Cassie turned from the window to call her producer, but the phone rang before she could pick up the receiver.

"Hello?"

"Miss Sheridan?"

"Speaking."

"There's a young man down here in the lobby who would like to speak with you. His name is Vincent Bayler."

Cassie's interest was piqued. He was a little devil, that one. What did he want?

"Tell him I'll be right down." It was safer to meet him in the lobby than run the risk of someone calling foul if she had the boy come up to her room.

CHAPTER
39

Charles and Etta Chambers wanted to be prepared, and they were doing everything the manual told them to do. Charles had packed up all their important papers and wrapped Etta's jewelry, storing it in the empty oven. He had moved the lounge chairs from the lanai into the living room while Etta packed a duffel bag with dry clothes and covered the computer and lamps with plastic bags. They would wait until the evacuation order actually came before covering the television. Until then the TV was their lifeline.

"Honey, you should be taking it easy after your surgery. I can do this," said Charles.

"I'm fine and it's all done." She patted the sofa cushion beside her. "Come, sit and watch the news with me."

"I don't think I have enough money. I'm going to the ATM," Charles declared, suddenly remembering one of the hurricane preparation instructions.

"Not now, dear. You can go in the morning."

"In the morning they might be out of money. I'll be right back."

Alone, Etta waited for the news to begin. She leaned forward at the opening story. That poor Mr. Sebastien. It was so sad.

But the follow-up report upset her even more. The hand that the cute boy had found on the beach yesterday morning belonged to a pornography actress.

Oh, my, she thought. *Wait until I tell Charles.* Etta went to the kitchen to pour herself a drink, really questioning their decision to move down here.

CHAPTER
40

Vincent paced up and down, keeping a darting watch between the elevator doors and his bike outside the lobby window. He had pedaled as fast as he could from Gideon's to the hotel, and his face was flushed and grimy.

He didn't know what else to do. He didn't want to go to his mother. She would be furious with him, he was sure of it. If he had turned over the ring in the first place, none of this would have happened.

The child was terrified.

He had gone too far this time, he thought, the anxiety mushrooming in his thin chest.

Was Gideon all right? He should've stopped and called an ambulance or something, but he'd just ridden as fast and hard as he could to get away, coming here to the lady reporter from big-time television. She'd know what to do far better than his mother would.

Trust your instincts, Cassie had said this morning. He hoped his instincts were right in coming here.

As the elevator doors slid open, Vincent suddenly remembered. *Mark.* He was supposed to be watching Mark.

The 7-Eleven had a telephone book, and the killer flipped through its worn pages. Barnes, Bates, Baxter . . . Bayler. He ripped out the page and closed the phone book.

Though he had pulled apart the old guy's ramshackle house, he hadn't found what he was looking for. Maybe the kid had the ring. The kid on the news who was identified as Vincent Bayler. And maybe that same kid had been the one hiding in the bathroom.

Suddenly ravenous, he grabbed a blueberry muffin from the display case, poured himself a cherry Slurpee, and made his way to the checkout counter. He drew out his wallet to pay.

"How do I get to Calle de Peru?" he asked, pulling at his expertly applied beard.

"Calm down. Calm down, Vincent," urged Cassie. "The first thing we have to do is call the police."

He didn't even try to talk her out of it. He knew she was right. Tears stung his eyes as he thought of poor Gideon, imagining his friend lying on the kitchen floor. He pictured a pool of blood surrounding a dead body, just like on television. But this wasn't make-believe, or even a bad dream.

Vincent gave Cassie Gideon's street address and listened as she made the call on the lobby phone. He couldn't imagine his mother talking to the police as matter-of-factly and calmly as Cassie did. As she held the phone to her ear, she mimed writing on a piece of paper and pointed to the front desk. Vincent went over and retrieved a pen and pad from the receptionist.

The reporter in Cassie scribbled down the name of the sheriff's deputy she spoke to and made a notation of the time. Next she picked up the house phone and punched a three-digit number. "Leroy, it's Cassie. I want to use the crew car."

* * *

She was already over an hour late, and Wendy couldn't wait any longer. The boss had called three times, finally threatening that if she didn't get her tail in there, she could look for another job. "Mark, honey, I'm sure Vincent will be home in a few minutes." She tried to keep her voice calm, although she wanted to wring Vincent's neck. "You'll be okay by yourself for just a little while, won't you?"

The child looked up from his half-eaten plate of macaroni and cheese and nodded solemnly.

"Okay, sweetheart. I'll lock the doors, and don't open them unless you are sure it's Vincent. I'll call you from work, but if anyone else calls, don't tell them you're here alone. Just tell them that your mother is in the shower and she'll call back when she gets out. Promise?"

"Promise, Mom."

Wendy gathered her purse and freshly washed apron and kissed Mark on top of the head. "Be a good boy."

"I will, Mommy."

Wendy pulled the front door firmly behind her and rattled the knob to make sure it was locked. Then she took off at a trot in the direction of The Old Salty Dog.

She didn't notice the polished car that was parked just down the street.

Cassie and Vincent loaded the bike into the back of the Jeep.

"My mother is going to kill me. I'm supposed to be watching my little brother while she goes to work. The last time she brought Mark to work she almost lost her job. He was coughing all over the place and grossing out the customers."

"Maybe you should call her." Cassie fished her cell phone out of her bag.

He didn't want to call, but he took the phone and counted the four rings until Mark picked up. "Mark. It's me, Vincent. Let me talk to Mom."

"She's in the shower. She'll call you back," the five-year-old answered, true to his promise.

"Okay, good," Vincent answered with relief. "Tell her I'm on my way home. I'll be there in about ten minutes."

Mark wasn't sure exactly how long ten minutes was, but it must have been fast because there was a knock on the door just a little while after he had hung up the phone.

"Vincent?" he called through the door.

"Police. Please, open the door."

His mother had told him that he should trust the police and always do what they said. The only experience Mark had had with the police was that nice man who came when he had the bad coughing attack. He wondered if it was the same policeman now.

His small hands fumbled with the button on the doorknob.

CHAPTER
41

"I'll come in with you, if you want," Cassie offered as they pulled up in front of the Baylers' house.

"Yeah, that would be good." Vincent didn't like admitting it, but after what had happened at Gideon's, there was no way he wanted to be left alone in his house to watch his little brother. He led the way up the walk. The front door was unlocked. What was the matter with Mark, anyway? He should know better. Mom was always lecturing them about keeping the door locked when she was gone.

"Mark, I'm home," called Vincent as he and Cassie entered the tiny living room. Cassie took in the tired surroundings, comparing them with her beautiful home in Alexandria. Hannah didn't know how good she had it.

The door off the living room was ajar, cool air from the bedroom escaping.

"Mark, you dope, you're supposed to keep the door closed," said Vincent with exasperation as he walked into the bedroom. The television was on. A half-empty glass of apple juice sat beside a coloring book and crayons spread on the floor. The beds were unmade and empty.

Vincent turned and muttered, "He must be in the bathroom." But only the sound of the faucet dripping into the worn tub filled the vacant room.

"Oh brother, I'm in big trouble now. My

mother must have taken him to work with her. The last time she had to do that, I couldn't sit down for a week."

Hannah had never had a hand raised in her direction, Cassie thought as she looked at Vincent's worried face. Maybe Cassie hadn't been there as much as many mothers were, but Hannah was never left by herself, and when she was there Cassie had tried to make up for it, making sure the child had everything. Maybe that was the mistake. Too many things, not enough uninterrupted time together. Letting sullen moods and tantrums go unchallenged. Making excuses for her daughter's behavior because of her own guilt about being away from home so much. "I'm sure your mother will understand when you explain everything."

"I doubt it," Vincent said glumly.

Cassie ached to put her arms around the boy, but she held back. "Would you like me to go with you and help explain things to her?"

Vincent's expression turned hopeful. "You'd do that?"

"Sure. Come on. Let's go."

CHAPTER
42

"You don't look like a policeman."

"Not all policemen wear uniforms."

Mark digested the information.

"This doesn't look like a police car."

"Well, it is."

"Does it have one of those lights?"

"No. It's an undercover car."

Mark looked out the window. "Hey, you said my mom wanted you to take me to her work," protested the little boy. "You were supposed to turn way back there."

The driver reached down and pushed the button that locked all the doors.

CHAPTER
43

He sure was glad he had such an under-standing wife. Danny Gregg had heard other guys on the force moaning that their wives complained when they had to work over-time. But not Colleen. They had already opened a college savings account for Rob-bie, and she looked at any extra money that came their way as an opportunity to make another deposit toward their son's educa-tion. They were both on the same team, she always told him. Though she wanted the family to be together whenever possible, Colleen would do her part and mind the home front while Danny was out earning a living.

There was going to be a good deal of overtime in the days ahead, thought Danny as he sped up to the curb. With the hurricane approaching, there would be a lot to do. The sheriff's department would be directing the evacuations that looked increasingly likely.

Deputy Gregg was the first to arrive at the scene, but he knew backup would be coming any second. He radioed his location to the desk. Then he got out of the truck and walked, hand on his holstered weapon, around the perimeter of the house. He could hear a siren growing closer.

He knocked forcefully on the screen door and called, "Police." Waiting just a few seconds, he pulled at the handle and walked through the porch and into the kitchen. A chair was turned on its side. All the cabinets and drawers were hanging open.

Danny heard a low moan. Turning in the direction of the sound, he saw the old man lying on the floor and hurried to him. White hair, a weathered face, now gray beneath its ruddy tan. Danny recognized the fisherman who'd been with the Bayler kid at the beach the day before.

"It's all right, old fella. It's going to be all right."

Blood oozed onto the cracked tiles as Danny heard the ambulance pull into the driveway outside. The old man's hand reached out, and Danny grabbed it, feeling the sticky blood.

"Vincent," came the whisper. The old man's last.

CHAPTER
44

Cassie recognized the frazzled blonde who had served her lunch that afternoon. Wendy was taking a dinner order, scribbling on a waitress's pad, smiling at her customers. The pleasant expression turned to one of alarm when she noticed her son standing on the deck. "What are you doing here? You're supposed to be home with Mark."

"I thought he was with you," said Vincent.

"No, I left Mark at home, waiting for you. You're in big trouble, buster. You were supposed to be home two hours ago." Wendy looked over Vincent's shoulder and saw her boss standing in the doorway. She bent down and hissed, "I'll take care of you later, young man. Now get home and take care of your brother!"

"But, Mom," Vincent pleaded.

"Don't 'but Mom' me. Get going." Wendy gave her son's arm a push.

Cassie intervened. "Mrs. Bayler, my name is Cassie Sheridan."

Wendy looked at her. "Do I know you?"

"Well, actually, I was here for lunch this afternoon."

"Oh yeah, that's right." With a quizzical expression on her face, Wendy looked from Cassie to her son.

"I'm a correspondent with KEY News. I met Vincent while I was working a story today," Cassie explained.

"I hope he didn't make a pest of himself."

"No. Not at all. But, to make a long story short, I just drove him home to your house, and, I'm sorry, but his brother wasn't there."

"Of course he's there. I left him there less than a half hour ago," Wendy said shrilly, fright beginning to register on her face.

"I'm sorry, Mrs. Bayler, I truly am. But Mark isn't there."

CHAPTER
45

Fortunately, the street was deserted. No one out to notice the crying little boy sitting in the car beside him.

He clicked the automatic door opener, pulled the car directly into the attached garage beneath the condo, and cut the motor. "Come on. Out we go."

"No. I want to go home. I want my mommy." The child began to cough.

"I have Coke inside," the driver coaxed. "Come on in and have some pop. It will make you feel better."

The boy's hacking increased.

"What's the matter with you? You have a cold?"

"No," he managed to get out. "I need a treatment."

"What kind of a treatment?"

"My pounder."

"What the hell is that?"

"You have to pound on my chest, or I won't be able to breathe."

"Jesus."

Consumed by his coughing, Mark let himself be guided from the car, through the garage, and into the condominium. The man pulled the boy by the arm, leading him to a small room. Metal hurricane shades were rolled shut on the windows. The man switched on a lamp.

"Now you sit down and rest," he said, indicating a studio couch. I'll go get you that Coke."

Mark heard a lock slide across the door in the hallway outside. Alternately, he whimpered and coughed while he looked around the room. The couch, a television set, some circus posters on the wall, and a dressing table with a mirror with lights around it.

On the top of the dressing table were bottles and tubes, brushes and powder puffs like Mommy's. At the thought of Mommy, Mark began to sob.

CHAPTER
46

For the second time in as many days, Deputy Gregg heard the address. "Child reported missing at 603 Calle de Peru."

The detectives going over the ransacked house heard the call, too. "Go on, Danny," said one of them with resignation. "We'll finish up here."

Danny gave a last glance at Gideon's now sheet-covered body and headed out the door. With a heavy heart, he drove the short blocks to the Baylers' house. He was well-trained for his job, but that was the first murder he had ever responded to. Just this morning he had almost wished that he had gotten the call to the murder up at Ringling. He thought he should have the experience. But after what he had just witnessed, he was glad he hadn't. He doubted he could ever get used to something like what he had seen back there. He didn't want to.

What was going on in their usually serene town?

Mrs. Bayler and her son Vincent were waiting outside the house, along with another well-groomed woman whom Danny didn't recognize. He listened as the mother, almost hysterical, told him what had happened.

"Okay, Mrs. Bayler. Let's not panic here. Mark could have wandered off. He might be safe at a neighbor's house right now."

"I told him not to leave the house," Wendy wailed. "Unlike his brother, Mark never disobeys me."

Vincent hung his head. Danny felt sorry for the kid.

"Look, I'm going to call to headquarters and get some help out here. We'll find your son, Mrs. Bayler. Try not to worry."

Wendy nodded and took a seat on the front stoop, burying her head in her hands. Cassie followed the deputy to the sheriff's department truck.

"Excuse me, Deputy. I'm Cassie Sheridan. I'm with KEY News. I made a call to the police about another matter this evening." She checked her notebook for Gideon's address.

Danny looked at her sharply. Back at headquarters they undoubtedly had registered the caller's name and address. "How was it that you made the call?"

Cassie tossed her head back toward Vincent, who sat on the steps with his arms around his mother. "The boy came to me and told me he had been there and that there was an intruder."

"Well, I'm sure we are going to want to talk to you and to Vincent about that. But right now, we have a child to find." Danny reached into the cab of the truck and made his radio call. Cassie waited until he was finished and then asked her last question. "What about the man who lived in the house?"

"He's dead, Ms. Sheridan. Stabbed to death. It looks like it was a robbery gone wrong. But from the looks of the place, I doubt there was too much to steal."

WEDNESDAY

August 21

CHAPTER
47

It was after midnight when Cassie dragged herself back to the hotel. The door-to-door search of the Baylers' neighborhood had proved fruitless. No one had seen Mark.

Wendy was so hysterical that she had needed to be sedated, and Cassie had stayed until the woman fell asleep. Cassie wasn't sure for whom she felt the most sorry. Wendy, the mother whose child was missing, or Vincent, the young boy who felt responsible for his brother's disappearance. The pain on Vincent's face was palpable. Cassie asked if he wanted her to stay with him, but Vincent refused the offer. "We'll be okay," he said in an attempt at bravery. "I can take care of my mom."

"You're sure? It's no big deal for me to stay and sleep on the couch."

"No. It's better if I just stay with my mother. I want to do at least something right today."

She left him sitting alone on the worn sofa.

Outside, Cassie stopped to talk with Deputy Gregg.

"We'll continue combing the neighborhood tonight. Tomorrow, when it gets light again, we'll be able to start dredging the nearby canals."

Cassie hadn't thought of the water. "Point me in the direction of the canal. I want to look for him."

The officer shook his head. "We've already patrolled the canal banks. Even with flashlights, it's too dark to do more tonight. You don't know the area, and we don't need to have anyone getting hurt."

"But we can't just let that little boy lie out there somewhere by himself all night," Cassie pleaded.

"There isn't much more we can do tonight," the deputy reiterated quietly. "Patrol cars will cruise the area overnight, and in the morning we'll intensify the search."

On the ride back to the hotel, Cassie felt nauseated. She had once lost Hannah while they were shopping at Tysons Corner. Somehow the toddler had wandered off, and Cassie clearly remembered running through the racks of clothing and yelling her daughter's name like a crazy woman. Within minutes Hannah had turned up in the arms of a salesclerk, but those minutes had seemed like an eternity. The memory could still make Cassie's stomach drop. She thanked God that she had never gone to bed not knowing where Hannah was.

Cassie didn't care if they were sleeping. She was going to call home.

Jim answered on the first ring.

"Did I wake you?"

"No. I'm reading a good mystery, and I'm staying up to finish it."

"How is Hannah?"

"She's fine."

"What's she doing?"

"What do you think she's doing, Cassie? She's in bed, asleep."

She supposed she shouldn't vent her

emotions to her estranged husband, but she and Jim had lots of years between them, and they were united in their love for their child. Cassie poured out the story of every parent's worst nightmare to the one person in the world who cared about her daughter as much as she did.

"Whoa. That's a rough one. God help that poor woman."

"Can you imagine losing Hannah, Jim?"

"No. I don't want to think about it. I can't imagine a world without her in it."

"Me neither." Her voice cracked. Cassie felt the tears coming, but she didn't care if he knew she was weeping. She was tired and vulnerable and alone in a hotel room hundreds of miles away from the ones she still loved.

"Don't cry, honey."

Honey. How she missed being called honey. How she missed their intimacy.

"I really messed things up, Jim, didn't I?"

"It takes two, Cassie."

She swallowed and plowed ahead. "Do you think there's any chance we could ever fix it?"

She heard a deep sigh through the phone line.

"Do you, Jim?" she pressed.

"I don't know, Cassie. I really don't. But I do know I need someone who's married to me, not her job."

It stung, but it was honest—and, at least, it wasn't a firm no.

Cassie fell asleep longing that they could make it right between them again.

CHAPTER
48

He couldn't sleep. The coughing coming from the locked room was driving him out of his mind. He wanted to get rid of the kid, but he needed that damned ring.

He pulled the folded page from the pocket of the shirt he'd draped over a chair in the corner of the room. If the mother answered, he would simply hang up. It was the boy that he wanted to talk to.

"Hello?"

Eureka.

"You want your little brother back?"

"Who is this?" Vincent demanded.

"You don't need to know who this is. All you need to know is, I have your brother and you have what it takes to get him back in one piece."

"What do you want?"

"I want that ring."

"What ring?"

"Don't play cute with me, kid. We both know what ring."

"I don't have any ring."

"Well, I don't have time to play games with you, boy. And your little brother doesn't have time for any games either."

"Is Mark all right?"

"Yeah, he's all right. But he's got some horrible cough."

"He has cystic fibrosis. He needs his medicine and his treatments."

"Well, it's up to you, Vincent. Turn over the ring and your brother can come home and get everything he needs."

"How do you know my name?"

"You're quite the little television star, kid. Look, I don't have any more time for chitchat. If you want to see your brother again, you'll turn over the ring."

There was silence from the other end of the phone line.

"Vincent?"

"Okay," said Vincent in a resolute voice. "I don't have it with me, but I can get it."

"When?"

"Tomorrow."

"All right. You know the Siesta Beach tennis courts?"

"Yeah."

"Wrap the ring in a plastic bag and tuck it underneath the trash can at the corner of the court. Have it there by noon."

"All right. Then will I get my brother?"

"You'll get your brother when I say so," he said sharply. "And, Vincent, you seem like a smart boy. Don't do anything dumb. If you tell the police about this, your brother's a goner."

He hung up the phone and went to his computer. He typed in "cystic fibrosis," and the search engine turned up over 45,000 websites. His resentment grew as it dawned on him that he had another complication he did not need.

Mark Bayler could die.

CHAPTER
49

It was already warm and humid on the New York City sidewalk as Range Bullock arrived at the Broadcast Center, earlier than usual. Yelena Gregory had given him a heads-up on what she wanted to discuss, and he wasn't looking forward to their conversation.

The news president's secretary wasn't in yet, and Range walked through the empty front office and knocked on Yelena's open door.

"Come on in, Range."

The executive producer took a seat in the chair Yelena indicated. She got right to the point. "Look, Range. We've got to make it official. We're going to name Valeria Delaney as justice correspondent. She's been doing the job for months, and she deserves it."

"I thought the plan was to wait until we saw how Cassie's lawsuit turned out."

Yelena tapped her pen on her large desk. "Yeah, well the plan has changed. Valeria's contract is up for renewal, and her agent says that ABC and CBS are interested in her. If she doesn't get the title, Valeria walks. We don't want to lose her, Range."

"What about Cassie?"

Yelena let out a heavy sigh. "It's an unfortunate situation. But that's the way it goes. I'm afraid, ultimately, we're going to have to let Cassie go"

"Who's going to tell her?" Range asked, remembering that he had been the one who had okayed her naming Maggie Lynch but still concerned about his own job security.

"I'll tell her about Valeria," answered Yelena, "but I'm not going to tell her she's out of a job until the lawsuit is settled."

CHAPTER
50

God was punishing him for lying yesterday. Today he really did feel miserable. When Brian called in sick again, the assignment editor would have none of it. SNN was hard-pressed to cover the story of the missing boy on Siesta Key. The bulk of the noon news broadcast would be dedicated to hurricane coverage. With evacuations ordered, the early morning assignment editor was scrambling to get his news crews on the roads to record Sarasotans boarding up their homes and getting out of the path of Giselle's impending wrath. Everyone had to come to work.

Brian arrived at the station and went straight to the news desk for his marching orders.

"You and Tony head out to Siesta and see what you can find," instructed the harried editor. "Get some pictures on the beach, take some shots of the traffic heading off the key, stop and get some man-on-the-street interviews. You know, the usual."

Brian nodded. The hurricane was not a run-of-the-mill story, but the fundamentals of covering it were the same as for any other assignment. His job was to get the pictures that would tell the story.

"And, Brian? Make a quick stop at 603 Calle de Peru and see what's going on there."

"What's the story?" asked the cameraman, trying to suppress his rising nausea.

"A five-year-old's been missing from the house since last night."

"Great," Brian responded dully. It was a helluva time for a kid to disappear. "The cops already have their hands full. I bet they can't have much manpower to devote to looking for the boy."

CHAPTER
51

"Cassie Sheridan on line three," announced the *Evening Headlines* desk assistant.

Range winced as he picked up the phone in the Fishbowl. "Hey, Cassie. What's going on?"

"It looks like this thing is going to hit here, Range. The authorities have ordered evacuations. Residents have to get out fast."

"All right. I'm going to list you guys above the line."

In her hotel room, Cassie held the phone to her ear while pulling on her jeans. "Okay, we're going to head out now." She added impulsively, "There is something else going on here, Range, that might turn out to be something we'd care about. There have been two deaths that could be connected to that boy band, the Boys Next Door. A woman who claims to have written their new song and a man who was at their concert here the night before last."

Range's interest was piqued. Viewers were notoriously intrigued by scandal surrounding entertainment figures. While the demographic audience of the evening news shows was significantly older than Boys Next Door fans, it could be a good story nonetheless. "See what you can find out," he answered. "Let me know."

Range hung up the phone feeling uncomfortable. He opened the bottle of Tums he kept on his desk and popped a tablet in his mouth. He had treated Cassie as if nothing was wrong. If he had been a better friend, he might have broken the news about Valeria Delaney before Yelena had a chance to do it. But he didn't want to tell her, and in the end Cassie Sheridan's career wasn't his responsibility. Or so he told himself.

Cassie made one more quick call before going downstairs to meet Leroy and Felix in the lobby.

"Hello?" answered the groggy voice.

"Mrs. Bayler? It's Cassie. Cassie Sheridan."

"Yes?"

"I just wanted to check if you had heard anything about Mark."

"Nothing."

What could Cassie say to that? "I'm so sorry." The response sounded so inadequate to Cassie's ears.

A sob came from the other end of the phone line.

"Would it be all right if I spoke with Vincent, Mrs. Bayler?" Cassie asked gently.

"He's not here. He said he wanted to go out and look for his brother. I couldn't stop him."

CHAPTER
52

Vincent waited for a pause in the thickening traffic on Ocean Boulevard, crossed over the macadam, and ran toward Gideon's house. On his path, palm fronds swayed against the ominous gray sky as rain began to fall.

The police had sealed the doors of the

run-down house with their yellow tape, but there was no one stationed to guard the property. Vincent hoped they were all out looking for Mark.

Gideon's battered Plymouth sat alone in the driveway. Vincent tried the doors, but they didn't budge. The cops must have locked the car.

He walked slowly to the bungalow, trying to psych himself up. If he could find the ring, he could get Mark back. He had to do what he had to do.

The boy swallowed hard and ripped the tape from the back door. He tried the rusty doorknob, but the police had locked that, too. Vincent pulled his Busch Gardens key chain from his pocket, separating out the key Gideon had given him.

The familiar smell of garlic greeted Vincent as he entered the kitchen. Gideon always said that garlic made fresh fish taste even better. He used garlic on just about everything, and the strong aroma had found its way into the thin cotton curtains on the windows and through to the upholstery on the furniture in the living room.

Vincent felt tears well in his eyes. He wouldn't be able to stand beside Gideon anymore as he fried up his prized daily catch at the old stove. There would be no more sea stories or tales of buried treasure. No one to run to show his latest find on the beach. He had lost his best friend.

Resolutely, Vincent wiped his palm across his wet cheek. He may have lost his buddy, but he sure as heck wasn't going to lose his brother. Not if he could help it.

And Vincent *could* help it—if he found that ring.

For the next half hour, he rummaged through all the places that the intruder and the sheriff's department had already searched, hoping against hope that they had missed something. They hadn't.

Where would Gideon have put the ring? Where would he have thought it would be safe? Vincent stood quietly in the middle of the kitchen and tried to think as he imagined his friend would think. Nothing special came to his mind. Absentmindedly, he walked to the door and looked out on the rear porch, cringing as he noticed Gideon's tacklebox lying on the floor. That old, battered box was Gideon's prized possession.

It was worth a try!

Vincent squatted beside the box and lifted the dented metal lid. In the special compartment, beneath the jumble of lures and hooks, he found what he was looking for.

CHAPTER
53

Warm rain slapped against their yellow rubber slickers as Cassie, Leroy, and Felix alighted from the crew car in the marina parking lot. While Felix unloaded the gear, Cassie and Leroy ran ahead toward the docks, scouting out targets of opportunity to obtain the best video material. Scores of sailboats and cabin cruisers rocked, vulnerable in the graying waters. Pelicans perched in determination on the wooden posts. Men in shorts and dock shoes and hooded rain jackets pulled and lashed and worked to secure their craft as the rain fell harder.

"You say this guy knows we're coming?" asked Leroy.

"Well, we didn't set up an exact time," Cassie answered, "but he told me yesterday that he would talk to us."

She wiped back a strand of wet hair from beneath her hood and squinted through the rain, spotting the marina owner's bright orange baseball cap. Jerry Dean stood at the end of the main dock talking to another man.

"There he is, Leroy." Cassie pointed. She headed out onto the dock, leaving Leroy behind. The wooden planks creaked beneath her sneakered feet.

"Jerry?"

The marina owner spun toward her, his brow furrowed, his mouth set in a grim, downturned line.

"Cassie Sheridan, from KEY News," she reminded him. "I know this is a very bad time for you," she apologized, "but could you talk to us for a few minutes?"

"Oh God, I don't know, lady. I'm up to my eyeballs here." He gestured loosely out at the churning water.

This was a part of her job that Cassie hated. Convincing people to be interviewed, cajoling them, when talking before the television camera was the last thing they had on their worried minds. It seemed like such an invasion of privacy. But human reaction was what made a riveting piece. It was the spice in the recipe of facts and images. "Just a few questions on what you're up against here, Jerry. I promise, it will be quick. Then, if it's all right with you, we'll take some shots of the marina and the boats."

Cassie shot an uncomfortable glance at the man who stood beside the marina owner, automatically noting how good-looking he was. He looked vaguely familiar, but she couldn't place him.

"All right," Jerry answered with resignation. "I told you I would, so I will. But let's do this fast."

Cassie beckoned Leroy and Felix out to the end of the dock. Felix clipped a wind guard on the microphone, handed it to Cassie, and hoisted his camera on his shoulder, fiddling with the focus. Cassie held up a blank page of her reporter's notebook for the cameraman to aim at while he adjusted the white balance.

"Go ahead," called Felix from behind the big camera. "Anytime you're ready."

Cassie held the microphone beneath her

mouth and asked her first question. "What are you anticipating here?" She swung the microphone to her interviewee.

Jerry sighed, rain peppering his face. "Well, the weather service has issued its watch for a wide belt up and down the west coast. I'm hoping that the hurricane doesn't hit us hard, but I'm preparing for the worst."

The microphone went back to Cassie's mouth. "What does that involve?"

"We're trying to tie up these boats as tight as we can. After that, it's in Mother Nature's hands."

Cassie recognized her sound bite, but she continued. "How many boats do you have moored here?"

"About two hundred."

"What do you think they're worth?"

Jerry paused to consider. "Millions."

"They're insured, aren't they?"

"Sure, owners insure their boats. But you never get it all back. And sometimes, after people go through something like this, they don't have the heart to buy another boat."

"So the ramifications are not good for your business," Cassie led.

Jerry looked at her with exasperation. "Of

course, the ramifications are bad for my business. It can take years to come back from something like this." He was at the end of his patience, and Cassie knew it.

"Okay. I think we have enough. Thank you for your time."

The camera clicked off.

Felix's camera recorded the seabirds huddled on the edges of the dock, the rain sliding off their oily wings; and thick ropes coiled around wooden piles, connecting expensive water craft to their moorings. The cameraman stopped repeatedly to wipe the rain from his lens as he shot video of the rocking boats from a half dozen vantage points.

"We should try to get an owner to talk to us," Leroy suggested.

Cassie scanned the area. The man who had been speaking with Jerry was watching them. Cassie walked over to him. She didn't bother introducing herself again. "You have a boat docked here?"

The man nodded. "That's mine. *The Eyes Have It.*"

Cassie looked in the direction the man's hand pointed. "Beautiful boat."

"Thanks. I hope it survives."

"Would you be willing to say just that for our camera?"

The man shrugged. "Sure, I guess so."

After the short interview, Cassie asked the man to state and spell his name so she would have the correct information for the identifying graphic that would be superimposed under his picture from the studio in New York.

"Harrison Lewis, M.D."

Cassie placed the face that she had first seen atop a tuxedoed body. "You were at the fund-raiser at the Ringling mansion the other night, weren't you?"

Lewis looked at her sharply. "Yes, I was. I noticed you, I think you noticed me. My friends call me Harry, by the way."

Cassie felt her cheeks grow warm. Busted. She was thankful when Felix interrupted.

"We have some good stuff, Cassie. It would be great to have some shots from another angle, though." The wiry cameraman shot a sly look at Harry. "From the water looking into the marina."

Cassie picked up on it. "I don't know how we are going to get that, Felix. There's a small-craft advisory posted. Boats aren't supposed to go out." She felt Harry staring at her.

"I could take you out," the doctor offered.

"You'd be willing to do that?"

"Yeah. Why not? I've sailed in worse than this. We'll just go out a little way, you can get your pictures, and we'll come right back. Nobody will be the wiser."

CHAPTER
54

Wendy was lying on the couch, and Deputy Gregg sat in the chair he had pulled up beside her. When Vincent, soaking wet, bounded through the front door into the living room, his mother's eyes brightened. But seeing no small figure following her older son, Wendy shrank back on the sofa in defeat.

"Go get a towel," she instructed dully, and returned her attention to the officer.

"I wish we could have someone here to stay with you, Mrs. Bayler. But this hurricane is using all of our staff. With the evacuations ordered, there's a lot to do," Danny apologized.

"I don't need anyone to stay with me. I need you all out there looking for Mark."

"We are, Mrs. Bayler. We are." Danny was uncomfortable with his own reassurances. A few guys were looking around for the missing five-year-old, but most of the sheriff's department resources were being directed at getting the thousands of islanders off the Sarasota keys. The kid couldn't have wandered off at a worse time. If he *had* wandered off.

"Mrs. Bayler, I hate to bring this up, but I have to. Many missing children cases turn out to be the work of an ex-spouse. Do you think there is any chance that Mark's father might have taken him?"

Wendy's mouth cracked into a leer. "That's rich. Vinny Bayler hasn't bothered with his kids for years. Hasn't bothered to see them, hasn't bothered to send any money to support them. He wasn't happy even when they were born. I doubt that he's all of a sudden gotten fatherly."

Danny cast a look at Vincent, who stood wide-eyed, listening to every word. Nice for a kid to hear that his father didn't want him.

"Just the same, do you know where we can get in touch with him?" asked the deputy.

"I have no idea. The last I heard, he was shacked up with some Cuban girl in Miami somewhere. I think he had a baby with her, too. Another child with his miserable blood."

At that Vincent walked into his bedroom and shut the door, locking it behind him.

With all his determination, Vincent pushed the stinging words from his mind. He couldn't afford to worry about his mother's cruel comments now. He had to concentrate on getting Mark back.

He was tempted to march back out there and tell Deputy Gregg about the call from the kidnapper. But he had watched enough television to know that going to the cops didn't mean everything would work out fine. The cops fouled up sometimes. They made mistakes. Kidnappers panicked. The abducted person died. The kidnapper had insisted that Vincent not go to the police, and Vincent wasn't going to.

He peeled off his wet T-shirt, tossed it on the floor, and pulled on a dry one. Lying down on Mark's bed, he could smell his brother on the pillowcase. When he got his brother back, he was going to be nicer to him. He promised. He felt around in the deep pockets of his shorts and patted the ring.

Television had also taught him that once the kidnapper got his ransom, there was no guarantee he'd give Mark back. Vincent was going to keep his side of the bargain. He had to make sure that whoever had taken his little brother was going to keep his.

The boy got up and opened his closet, taking out the cardboard box that was home to his shell collection. He emptied the contents on the floor. He scooped Mark's plastic prescription bottle from the top of the dresser and wrapped the cord around the electric pounder that still lay on the floor from the last time Mark had used it. He didn't want to think how long it had been since Mark had had a treatment, didn't want to imagine how congested his brother must be by now.

He placed the medicine and the pounder in the box. Then he pulled off the cover of one of Mark's coloring books and began to write on the back of it. He was reading over what he had written when there was a knock on the door.

"Mark?" called his mother.

He folded the paper, put it in the box, and slid everything under the bed.

"Mark." Her voice was stronger this time.

"Coming."

He unlocked the door and opened it.

"I'm sorry, Vincent. I shouldn't have said all that stuff about your dad in front of you."

Well you did, Vincent thought, *and you can't take it back.* Instead, he answered, "That's okay."

He studied his mother's face as she stood in the doorway. She suddenly looked a lot older to him. Old and very tired. He felt sorry for her and momentarily guilty that he was such a burden to her. But, hey, he didn't ask to be born.

"That deputy says we should evacuate, but I told him that I'm not leaving this house until I have Mark back. What if he came home and nobody was here?"

She turned and walked back to the couch, not waiting for her son's answer. As she lowered herself onto the frayed cushions, she remembered. "That newswoman called. She left her cell phone number." Wendy thrust her chin in the direction of the kitchen.

Vincent picked up the slip of paper from the counter and studied the number before putting it in the breast pocket of his T-shirt.

CHAPTER
55

Even before she climbed into the boat, Cassie was worried about it.

She hadn't experienced it in years, but she hadn't forgotten going out onto the Chesapeake Bay on a rented boat that time when Hannah was little. It was a day far calmer than this one, but in the middle of their sail she had felt nausea more intense than any she had ever known.

Since then Cassie had kept away from small boats. She was tempted to tell Leroy and Felix to go on without her, but she didn't want to wimp out. After all, this boat was larger than the one she had been on then. And maybe that seasickness had been just a one-time thing.

Harrison Lewis had steered them out only ten minutes into the choppy water when she began to feel it. The color drained from her face and her knuckles turned white as she gripped the edge of the boat.

The men were enjoying the ride, probably imagining themselves as sailors of long ago, bravely facing the elements. They shouted and laughed as water sprayed their faces. "I'm getting great stuff," Felix called from behind his camera.

Cassie had some vague memory about instructions to pick a spot on the horizon and focus on it. She tried, but it did no good. The feeling grew more intense.

"How you doing back there?" Harry shouted over his shoulder.

"Not great," she managed to call back.

"Seasick?"

She couldn't get an answer out. She swung her head and hung it over the side. It was either that or vomit all over the floor of the pristine sailboat.

Cassie turned back to see Leroy trying to keep a smirk off his face. *Macho man.*

The doctor was far more solicitous. "You feel any better now?" he asked.

"Not really." She wanted to die.

"There are some pills down in the head. Why don't you go and get them?"

Anything for some relief. She had a story to cover and a script to write. She had to feel better. Cassie eased herself down the ladder.

Inside the tiny bathroom she pulled open the drawer. Beneath a tube of toothpaste, a few toothbrushes, a bottle of mouthwash, and a container of aspirin she recognized an amber pharmacy bottle. She read the typed instructions and popped the prescribed amount in her mouth, washing it down with a sip of water from the miniature faucet over the sink.

As she fastened the cap back onto the container, Cassie noticed the name of the person for whom the medicine had been prescribed.

Merilee Quiñones.

CHAPTER
56

Hurricane or no hurricane, Webb planned to stop for his Krispy Kreme fix on the way to the studio. Between the loss of Merilee and the abysmal shoot with Gloria and Van yesterday, he was under a lot of stress. He deserved the treat.

When he reached the gas station that sold the addictive donuts, the lot was full of cars gassing up in preparation for the storm, and motorists waited in a line that stretched down the highway for their turns at the pumps. Even for a Krispy Kreme he wasn't going to wait in that mess. His ill temper increased as he battled the traffic that inched along the road, giving him more time to think and stew. He tapped impatiently on the steering wheel as he mentally scrolled through his list of problems.

The police wanted to talk to him about Merilee.

Lou-Anne was apoplectic at the likelihood that publicity about the porn star's death would lead investigators to Web of Desire Productions and that her friends would come to know what her husband really did for a living.

He needed *Velvet Nights in Venice* to be a success. His lifestyle and his ego demanded it. But if what they had shot yesterday was any indication, the industry reviews of this video were going to suck.

The windshield wipers swept back and forth. Webb switched on the radio and listened to the announcer's voice listing local evacuation centers. This damn hurricane was another freakin' bummer. Even if the house and studio survived the ripping winds and pounding rain, you weren't out of the woods. The storm surge afterward could do the most savage damage of all, flooding out structures and ruining furnishings and equipment.

Webb pulled into the studio parking lot thinking how, in the end, it always was about money. Even his precious Merilee, whom he had so carefully cultivated, got greedy, demanding a cut of the profits. He had tried to string her along for as long as he could, promising her the world but never delivering.

Now, he didn't have to.

CHAPTER
57

Harry held Cassie's arm, helping her off *The Eyes Have It.* "There you go. Back on solid ground."

Cassie managed a wan smile.

"Thanks a lot, Doc," said Leroy extending his hand. "Watch *KEY Evening Headlines* tonight and you'll see the fruits of your labors."

"If I'm home, I'll do that." He shook the producer's hand. "I'm hoping I can avoid evacuating."

Leroy and Felix started down the dock ahead of her. Cassie, though she felt too rotten to do it, knew she should seize the opportunity to learn anything she could about the potential story she had pitched to Range on the phone this morning. She held back to talk to the boat's skipper. "I'd like to ask you about something totally unrelated to the hurricane," she began.

"Shoot." Lewis looked happy to oblige.

"I noticed the motion sickness prescription had the name Merilee Quiñones on it, the woman whose hand was found on the beach."

The pleasant expression changed.

"Yes. I knew Merilee."

"May I ask how well?"

"Well enough to have her on my boat."

"Do you have any theories about what happened to her?"

Harry paused, as if trying to choose just the right words. "Merilee was a gorgeous young woman, and she could be a lot of fun. We had some great times together. But she wanted a future and I wasn't going to give her one."

Cassie waited. He still hadn't answered her question.

"I don't know what happened to Merilee, but I'll tell you this: she ran with a fast crowd and was into a lot of different things." He hesitated before continuing. "The porn didn't sit well with me, but she didn't want to give it up. That tells you something about her, doesn't it? A girl like that is destined for trouble."

Harry watched Cassie's back as she walked down the dock.

How incredibly stupid of him not to have remembered that Merilee's name was on the prescription bottle. He had been so damned eager to play the shining knight coming to the aid of the beautiful television reporter.

He hoped his responses to Cassie's questions had hit the right chord. It was obvious to the reporter that Merilee had been on his boat. There was no use denying it. The television and newspaper reports already had revealed the way Merilee made her living, so there was no sense in avoiding the topic.

For the sake of his public and professional life, Harrison Lewis, M.D., had gone to great lengths to keep his relationship with Merilee Quiñones a secret. Now, Cassie Sheridan knew about it.

CHAPTER
58

Merilee was gone, and she was never coming back. On the one hand, that was a relief. On the other, it was a real worry. It wouldn't take long for the police to find their way to his door.

Van paced the living room of his condo, oblivious to the pounding rain outside. The porn awards he'd won in his salad days seemed to mock him from his bookcase. Pictures of a swarthy, muscular, glowering youth haunted him from their frames. No longer would he have to suffer Merilee's snide comments about his prowess, her taunts reminding him that his best days were behind him. The things that were truest hurt the most. For Van, hurt equaled rage.

He'd always had a problem controlling himself, even as a little kid. His mother, if he had to call the bitch that, was forever sending him to his room. At first, only when he answered her back or talked in church. Later, when she caught him in lies or got calls from school about his cutting up in class and cheating on tests.

His mother was the guilt queen, always crying and pleading and begging him to tell her where she had gone wrong. How the hell was he supposed to know? He just did what came naturally. But she couldn't accept the way he was. She kept dragging him to church to pray for his soul.

At sixteen, he finally made his escape. But not before he hauled off and hit her. It was just one good swipe across her pious face, but God, did it feel right. Years of frustration and rage culminated in that hard swat. Van left her weeping on the kitchen floor, and he never looked back.

At first, it had been rough for a teenager on his own. With no high school diploma and no one to look out for him, he'd gotten a job flipping burgers and slept at a homeless shelter that was run, ironically, by a church. But that place had too many rules and regs. Residents had to be in by ten o'clock each night. It was as bad as being at home.

He took to hanging around a local gym,

eventually getting a job as a towel boy. The owner let him work out when things were slow. Within a couple of months, Van's body was hard, his muscles well defined.

Van lied about his age when he went for his next job, a performer at Ladies Night, one of those joints where women came to ogle and cackle as oiled studs danced and thrust themselves in their faces. It didn't take long before Van became the club's most popular attraction.

He enjoyed the adulation. Unlike his mother, those women adored him, and they showed it in the bills they stuffed in his low-slung belt. He could afford the rent on a small place of his own.

For a couple of years he danced his ass off, until the owner of the club approached Van with a proposition. He knew a guy who shot adult films. He was always looking for new talent. The owner would introduce Van to Webb Morelle, and if it worked out, Van could throw a couple of bucks the owner's way. For Van, one of the best reasons for giving it a go was the knowledge that his mother would hate the idea so much.

Van sat back in his leather recliner and surveyed his surroundings. Twenty years of filmmaking wasn't a bad run. It had paid for this condo, the boat docked down at the marina, the late-model cars he liked to drive fast, and the trips he liked to take. He had some money in the bank. But not enough to live on for long if he lost his source of income.

That was why Merilee had gotten to him with her barbs. She had struck him where he lived, where he was most vulnerable. Once you've lived in a homeless shelter, you don't want to go back.

His mistake was that he had hit her.

While Webb had convinced Merilee to drop the charges, somewhere the sheriff's department would still have a record of her complaint.

He rose from the chair and walked to the bathroom, where he opened the medicine cabinet and pulled out a small envelope and a fresh razor blade. He made the preparations on a hand mirror and sniffed the line of white powder.

Immediately, Van felt better. More powerful, more invincible. Younger. He grabbed his keys and went out for a little ride in the rain.

CHAPTER
59

How many shots of backed-up traffic could you get? Brian knew he had more than enough pictures of bumper-to-bumper cars heading off Siesta Key. He had parked the SNN microwave van at the side of Ocean Boulevard and stationed himself in the rain, shooting while Tony Whitcomb interviewed motorists who had nothing to do but wait and complain.

"It's a good thing we got an early start. I'd hate to see what this will be like later in the day."

"This is a nightmare. There should be more ways to get off this island."

"I hope all these people aren't going to the same evacuation center. There won't be enough room."

The plan was for Tony to write a short script that would be fed back to the station from the van via microwave, along with all the video Brian had gotten. The piece would be edited at the studio. To make their slot on the noon news, they should feed their material in by eleven o'clock.

"The desk wants us to see if we can get some pictures at the house of that missing kid," Tony reminded Brian as he began to scribble out his script on a notepad.

"Oh yeah, right." Brian hoped his queasy stomach wouldn't get the better of him.

The van traveled against the heavy traffic.

"The cops better let us use our press passes on the way back," said Tony. "There's no way I'm going to wait in all this traffic."

Their lane was deserted, and within minutes they drove through the heart of Siesta Village and onto Calle de Peru.

"It never ceases to amaze me how well you know this area," said the reporter. "I've been living here for years and I wouldn't have found this street."

"I checked a map before we left the station," Brian muttered. "I like to know where I'm going."

The street was quiet. Many of the houses' windows were boarded up, but not those at 603. It was as if the owner didn't think there was anything worth protecting in the shabby bungalow.

"You want to knock on the door and see if you can get somebody to talk to you?" asked Brian.

Tony glanced at his watch. "I don't have time. I've got to get this piece written. Let them voice-over the pictures of the house for the noon show. If we get a chance, we can come back later."

Brian nodded. He got out of the van, unloaded his camera, and got to business. He was ready to put the camera back in the truck when the front door of the house opened.

A boy carrying a cardboard box under his arm walked down the front steps. He paused when he spotted the conspicuous news van.

Tony saw the boy, too. The reporter rolled down his window and called to Brian. "Hey, that's the kid from the beach the other day. The one who found the hand!"

They both knew what to do. Tony bounded from the truck, Brian got up to speed, and they descended on the kid.

But Vincent would have none of it. He refused to answer the questions the reporter threw at him. He walked on toward the beach having learned his lesson. Talking to the television people could get you in trouble.

CHAPTER
60

Leroy snapped his cell phone closed after his conversation with New York. "We should have all the pictures of evacuation traffic we need from SNN. They've booked a window to feed in that material directly from the station this afternoon."

"So New York's going to edit?" asked Felix.

"Yep."

"Fine with me." Not having to edit the piece gave the cameraman one less big thing to worry about.

Leroy turned to Cassie, who sat alone in the backseat. "So we've got the marina stuff and the evacuations. New York is also going to do a telex interview with someone from the National Hurricane Center that we can throw in. It would be nice to have another element. Any suggestions?"

Cassie's mind hadn't been on Giselle. She was thinking of her conversation with Harrison Lewis, which led to Merilee, which led to Vincent and his missing brother. She had made sure her cell phone was on, hoping Vincent would call her back, but he hadn't. She hesitated to call the Bayler house again. If Mark hadn't turned up, Cassie didn't want to put Wendy in the position of having to say it another time.

"Earth to Cassie Sheridan. Hello?"

"I'm thinking, Leroy. I don't know. You want to go to an evacuation center and get some pictures and interviews there?"

"Good idea. That's why they pay you the big bucks, Cassie."

She couldn't stand the smug sarcasm in his voice.

CHAPTER
61

"They want us to do the live stand-up on Siesta Beach," Tony complained after talking to the noon broadcast producer.

"What's the difference? We're already soaked." He was really going to be sick now.

Brian steered the microwave truck past the tennis courts into the deserted public lot and parked as close as he could to the beach. He busied himself making the connections necessary to transmit back to the station. Brian watched the audio levels and adjusted the dials as Tony recorded his track. Then the cameraman fed the evacuation pictures they had shot along with the video of the Bayler house.

"Maybe we should go back after the live shot and try to get the mother to say something. We could make a piece with that for the six o'clock show," Tony mused.

"Whatever." Brian grimaced. "Who's really

going to care, though? Tonight is going to be all hurricane, all the time."

"I'm starving," Tony declared as they waited until it was time to go out for the stand-up.

"A ginger ale sounds good to me. There better be somewhere open around here."

Tony began one of his standard harangues about what he was in the mood for, a dripping meatball sandwich and golden onion rings topping his list. Brian plotted how he would demand that the assignment editor let him go home. Neither one of them noticed the boy sliding the box beneath the trash can next to the tennis courts.

CHAPTER
62

It was after 12:30 when he parked a few blocks from the tennis courts and walked the rest of the way. He didn't need anyone to be able to identify his vehicle, conspicuous in an empty parking lot.

The soggy, sand-coated package that he pulled from beneath the trash can was bigger and much heavier than expected. Inside, the ruby ring was nowhere to be found.

The rotten kid had double-crossed him.

How dare he? How dare the kid dictate how it was going to be? He felt the rage pulse inside him as he reread the directions written in immature handwriting.

You want the ring. I want my brother and I have to be sure that you are really going to give him back. We need to swap. Come to the Old Pier at 6 o'clock tonight with my brother. When I see Mark, then I'll give you the ring. Here is Mark's medicine and the machine he needs to help him breathe. He can tell you what to do with it. You better take good care of my little brother. If anything happens to him, you are in BIG trouble.

Vincent Bayler

He stuffed the note back into the box and ran from the parking lot. The kid had big ones to threaten him like this. The little bastard had no idea who he was dealing with.

CHAPTER
63

Vincent could feel his heart pounding as he waited to come out from his cramped hiding place. The slits between the wooden boards that rimmed the outdoor beach showers had provided a good spot for spying.

He wanted to make sure Mark's medicine and pounder were going to get to him. He'd hoped that he would be able to see what kind of car the man was driving, maybe even get the license number. He hadn't expected the man to come on foot.

He wished he could have been closer and gotten a look at the man's face. But there had been nowhere else to conceal himself.

All in all, though, his mission had been a success. At least now he knew that Mark could get the stuff he needed.

CHAPTER
64

It was busy. A steady stream of customers came through the doors of the 7-Eleven, emptying the shelves of juices and sodas and cookies and crackers. Hurricanes were good for business. The young clerk had been occupied all morning, ringing up purchases, refilling the Slurpee machine, restocking the shelves. The owner called to say he should close up by one o'clock and get out of there. It couldn't come soon enough.

"This is all you have left?" asked a man with a too-perfect haircut, holding out a pair of plastic-wrapped tuna sandwiches.

"Sorry. That's it, mister."

"Pathetic. I waited in the line for this?" Brian wasn't going to be happy with these lousy things. Tony dreaded going back out to the truck with these paltry offerings.

The conscientious clerk felt somehow responsible. "We have some donuts left," he offered, thrusting his chin toward the display cabinet.

"Forget it."

The clerk watched as the man opened his wallet, revealing a picture ID card embossed with big letters. SNN.

"You with the news?" the clerk asked.

The man's face brightened. "Yeah, I'm Tony Whitcomb."

"Covering the hurricane, huh?"

"Yeah, that's right," came the self-important response. "The hurricane and that missing Bayler kid."

The clerk looked puzzled. "What Bayler kid?"

"A five-year-old that lives a couple of blocks from here has been missing since last night."

"Wow. I didn't know that. That's really bad." The clerk turned to ring up the next customer.

It wasn't until he had locked the doors of the store that the clerk had a chance to think of it. The weird guy who came in last night. The one who thought no one saw him rip out the page from the phone book. The one who asked how to get to Calle de Peru.

The clerk went to the phone book and paged through to the B's. The page where Bayler would have been listed was gone.

CHAPTER
65

Islanders arrived at the evacuation center, staking out their territory. Sleeping bags, air mattresses, and cots lined the floors of the high school cafeteria, gymnasium, class-rooms, and hallways.

"I suppose this is where we should come if it gets too bad tonight," Leroy mused aloud. "Maybe we should mark out our spot."

"If you want to," answered Cassie without enthusiasm. She wouldn't be sleeping, she'd be working. Felix would be shooting, she would be interviewing evacuees and writing a script for *KEY to America*. The morning broadcast would undoubtedly want a piece. Only Leroy might have a chance to get some rest.

It didn't take long to get what they needed for their story. Felix took some general shots of the evacuees and Cassie did a few interviews. They were leaving the building when Cassie's pager went off. The tiny screen told her to call Yelena Gregory in New York.

She tried to keep her fingers steady as she pushed the numbers on her cell phone. Maybe there was some news on the lawsuit. Maybe a settlement had been reached. "Cassie Sheridan answering Yelena's page."

"Yes, just a moment please."

Yelena came on the line quickly. "How's it going down there, Cassie? You keeping dry?"

Cut the small talk, Yelena, Cassie thought with impatience. *You know it and I know it. News presidents don't call to discuss the weather.*

"We're doing okay, but it looks like it's going to get rough."

"I know you'll do a great job."

"Thanks, Yelena."

"Uh, Cassie. I have something I want to

tell you before you hear it from someone else."

"Something happen with the lawsuit?"

"No. No news on that front."

Cassie's mind raced. If it wasn't the legal nightmare, then what? "Well, what is it, Yelena?" She braced herself.

"Cassie, I'm sorry. I truly am. But we've felt it important to officially name Valeria Delaney as justice correspondent. She's been doing a great job and she's earned it."

Cassie tried to control her voice. "You told me that you were going to hold off, and when we finished with the lawsuit, I could be coming back to Washington."

"I'm sorry, Cassie."

"I hear you saying you're sorry, Yelena, but sorry doesn't cut it. That's my job. This isn't fair."

The argument about fairness sounded childish to her own ears. Fairness had nothing to do with anything anymore.

CHAPTER
66

This was the first kid he had ever seen who was eager to take his medicine.

"I have to lay down on my side and you have to hold the pounder to my chest."

The machine did its work as the child coughed up phlegm into one Kleenex after another.

"Who gave you my medicine? Did my mommy bring it?"

"No. Your brother gave it to me."

"Vincent? Vincent brought it?"

"Yeah, Vincent."

"Where is he? I want to see him."

"You'll see him, don't worry."

"When?"

"When I say so. Now be quiet."

The little boy began to cry. "I want my mother." The coughing increased, racking the small body.

"Look, kid, try to relax. You're going to see your mommy. I promise. But until we can get to her, you've got to do what I tell you."

Mark wiped at his swollen eyes.

"Why do you have all that makeup? That's for ladies."

"Not always. Men wear makeup in the movies and on television."

"Are you on television?"

"No."

"Then why do you have it?"

He answered the boy with another question. "Ever been to the circus?"

"Yes, my mother took me." Mark looked like he was going to start bawling again.

"Remember the clowns?"

Mark shook his head up and down.

"Well, what do you think? You think those were their real faces? Of course not. They were wearing makeup."

"So, you're a clown?"

"On the inside, kid. On the inside."

For as long as he could remember, all he had ever really wanted was reassurance that he was attractive, acceptable, lovable. He had found none in the house where he grew up.

There was no touching in his house. No

cuddling, no caressing, no good-night kisses. Even discipline was meted out without the touch of the human hand. A leather belt did that, or a yardstick, or the back of his mother's hairbrush.

He watched the boy lying on the studio couch. The child was breathing better now, the coughing less frequent.

"You ever get in trouble, kid?"

Mark look puzzled. "Whaddya mean?"

"Does your mother ever hit you?"

"No," answered the child. "But she hits my brother sometimes," he offered, wanting to please his captor.

"What does she hit him with?"

"Her hand."

The feelings inside were pushing, pushing to the surface. He needed to do it. He needed some release. "Come here, kid. Come on over here."

Mark got up from the couch and took the seat at the makeup table.

"How 'bout I make you up as a clown?"

"Really?"

"Yeah."

He drew and painted and powdered the small, soft face, remembering that first clown.

The one at the circus he had begged his father to take him to for his birthday when he was just a little bit older than the boy who sat before him now. He could still remember his excited anticipation of that rare outing with his dad. The terror he felt when he had wet his pants in the circus stands. His father's disgusted expression, the hissed threat of what would happen when they got home.

In the circus ring, the clown had continued his antics, the grinning face mocking his already total humiliation.

CHAPTER
67

Screw KEY News. She'd had it.

She had devoted her professional life to the organization and had sacrificed a good deal of her personal life as well. Somehow Cassie had thought her loyalty would be returned. If she played by the rules, gave it her all, surely KEY News would do the right thing by her.

You fool. The fact of the matter was that everyone was expendable. You were useful as long as you were useful, but when things got too difficult or another option better suited their purposes, you were history.

They could argue that they paid you for services provided and they had every right to decide how they wanted to staff the news division. That was surely true. But Yelena had promised that they weren't going to hang Cassie out to dry. KEY News was going to stick by their award-winning correspondent. By naming Valeria Delaney to the Justice Department beat, KEY News was in fact announcing that it was leaving Cassie Sheridan behind.

Cassie hated herself for her naïveté. Or had it been wishful thinking? She had gone docilely to Miami when they told her to, hoping that they would manage things, expecting them to take care of her. That had been a huge mistake. *For a smart girl, you've been pretty damned stupid. You should have known you have to take care of yourself.*

On the ride back to the hotel from the evacuation center, Cassie stared out the window at the pounding rain and devised her plan. She'd be damned if she was going to roll over and play dead. She was going to show them, and herself, that she was one of the best reporters KEY News ever had.

In record time she pounded out her script on the laptop. She showed it to Leroy and then e-mailed it to the Fishbowl. While waiting for approval, Cassie went back to her room and fished the business card from her purse.

Sarge Tucker answered on the second ring. "What can I do for you?"

"I'd like to ask you a couple of questions."

"About?"

"The Boys Next Door and 'Nobody Knows.'"

"All right. Why not? But I'd prefer talking in person."

Cassie looked out the window, calculating that she still had to record her track and, later, do the live stand-up from the hotel balcony. "I can't get away right now. Any chance you can come to me?"

"In this mess? You've got to be kidding."

She held out the carrot. "I've heard that Merilee Quiñones was claiming that she wrote 'Nobody Knows.'"

"Where are you?" There was resignation in his voice.

"The Inn by the Bay—it's on Tamiami. There's a Denny's downstairs."

CHAPTER
68

The tranquilizers had worked. Dozing on the couch, Wendy awoke to the sound of a crash at the window. She pulled herself up and looked outside. A giant palm frond lay on the grass at the base of the house.

"Vincent?" she called out.

The sound of the howling wind was the only response.

"Vincent," she demanded, checking his empty bedroom.

Where was he now? She was going to kill that kid.

She saw the note on the kitchen counter.

Mom,
Don't worry. I'll be back soon.
                                    Vincent

What was the matter with him? He knew that she was worried sick about Mark. It was just like Vincent, running off, not thinking of her feelings.

She went back to the window and looked out again at the raging storm. Where could Vincent have gone to in this? Her mind went the natural next step. Vincent might drive her absolutely crazy, but she wouldn't be able to bear it if anything happened to her other son.

Cassie recorded the track that Felix would feed to New York.

"I'll be downstairs in the restaurant if you need me."

Denny's was deserted save for the man who sat in the corner. A dripping raincoat was draped on the chair beside him.

"Thanks for coming."

"I didn't have much of a choice, did I?" Sarge looked out the plate-glass window at the raging storm. "I should be at the evacuation center. Not here, defending myself against a baseless charge."

Cassie waited.

"How did you hear that Merilee claimed to have written 'Nobody Knows'?"

"I have my sources," said Cassie, thinking of the overheard conversation at the Ringling party, "and I'm not going to reveal them."

Sarge didn't have to know how vague her information was or that she was on a fishing expedition.

"Well, she was lying. Merilee didn't write 'Nobody Knows.' I did."

"That's a hard thing to prove, isn't it?"

The promoter shrugged. "Maybe, but I think I would have won if we went to court."

"But now you won't be going to court, will you? Merilee's not around to take you there."

Sarge picked up a napkin and wiped his damp brow. "Look"—he sighed—"I know it looks bad. A woman claims she wrote my song, a song that stands to make big, big money, and now that woman turns up dead. But, believe me, Merilee had a lot of irons in the fire. She was a real operator, and she made enemies along the way. I'll admit it. I'm not sorry Merilee's out of the picture, but I know I'm not the only one."

"Care to name names?" Cassie opened up her notebook.

"Her boss at the porno place for one. Webb Morelle at Web of Desire Productions couldn't have been too happy that she was demanding some of his action."

"And you know this, how?"

"Merilee told me. We were neighbors, you

know. She used to come over and we'd drink some wine and she'd run her mouth off about all her big plans. She had delusions of grandeur, that one." Sarge shook his head. "My mistake was I played 'Nobody Knows' for her before I had it copyrighted, never thinking that she would claim it as her own. I should have known better."

Cassie wanted to steer the conversation back. "Who else was Merilee on the outs with?"

"She couldn't stand that actor she had to work with. Van something or other. And by the looks of the welt on her arm she showed me one time, he wasn't too fond of her either."

"Anyone else?"

Sarge thought a moment. "Well, there was one poor slob I felt sorry for. I can't remember his name. From the sound of it, he had fallen for her hard. But she was just using him. She had her cap set for some eye doctor, and she was stringing this other clod along as a backup in case the doctor didn't come through."

The doctor must have been Harry Lewis, thought Cassie. Who was the clod?

CHAPTER
70

The late afternoon sky was dark and ominous. Vincent had to push himself through the wind and sheets of rain, stopping at the worst gusts to grab hold of a tree or street sign.

At the beach, roaring waves crashed on the Old Pier. As Vincent looked out at the concrete structure, Gideon flashed through his mind. All the hours they had spent together on the pier. All the good times they had had. No more.

If only he hadn't found this stupid ring!

Vincent patted at his rubber slicker, feeling the tiny bulge from the zippered pocket inside the jacket. The ring was there, safe and sound. He was going to keep his side of the bargain. This guy better keep his.

The boy waited.

He drove toward Siesta Key with Mark strapped into the front seat beside him. Safe enough. With the dark skies and the drenching rain, nobody was going to notice the boy.

"We're going home?" the five-year-old asked, recognizing familiar landmarks through the rain.

"Yeah, we're going to meet your brother."

It was going to be a relief to get rid of this sickly kid. Sweet or not, let him be somebody else's problem.

But as the car approached the North Bridge, his anticipation turned to panic. Police cars and barricades blocked the entrance.

Absolutely no one was being allowed on Siesta Key.

"Someone called us with something, Mrs. Bayler. The clerk at the 7-Eleven says a man came in early last evening and asked directions for Calle de Peru."

Wendy digested what Deputy Gregg's words could mean. "You think this man might have come and taken Mark?"

"It's a possibility we have to look at. Has anyone called?"

"No. Only a couple of hang-ups. How are you going to find this guy?" Wendy demanded.

Danny wished he knew. The clerk had described a man of medium build with a beard and grayish hair. But the kid had said there was something not quite right about the guy's appearance, though he couldn't put his finger on what it was. Danny suspected a disguise of some sort. "We're doing everything we can, Mrs. Bayler," he tried to reassure her. "In the meantime, you and Vincent have to get off this island."

"Absolutely not. There's no way I'm going, especially if someone has Mark and could be calling."

The sheriff's deputy understood. If Robbie was missing, he wouldn't leave either. "Well then, at least let us take Vincent to the evac center."

"That might be a good idea," Wendy admitted, "if Vincent was here for you to take."

CHAPTER
72

The furious gust blew him to the sand, pinning him there. Vincent struggled to get up but was blown down again and again. He managed to crawl toward the road, finding partial shelter under a boarded-up beach house perched on metal pilings. He huddled beneath his rainjacket, wiping the stinging water from his eyes, the wet, gritty sand from his face. How long had he been waiting?

He peered through the torrential sheets of rain, searching for some kind of movement. Car lights or a human figure. Two human figures, he hoped, one grown, one small. Instead, the only activity was the ceaseless crashing of the white-capped waves smashing onto the shore.

How was the guy going to see him beneath this house? He had to get out there and stand in a spot where he would be visible. With head tucked, he headed out again.

Each step took all his strength, planting his thin legs as firmly as he could into the sand for support against the punishing wind. When he reached the pier, Vincent was exhausted. Still, he clung to the hope that the man who had Mark would come. When he came, he'd have to be able to find him. If Vincent could climb on top of the pier, the guy would surely be able to spot him.

He hoisted himself up onto the concrete shelf. His rubber coat flapped against his body as he turned his back on the turbulent water, searching the dark beach for a sign of the man.

At the next gust of wind, Vincent felt himself propelled forward and his feet skid along the slick cement, struggling, in vain, to keep his balance.

CHAPTER
73

Hurricane Giselle was slated as the lead story on *Evening Headlines.* Felix was downstairs in the parking lot, manning the satellite truck. Cassie stood, miked up and ready, at the door to the hotel balcony.

"When we're through here, we're getting ourselves to the evacuation center," Leroy ordered, watching the boats tossing like bath toys in the marina across the road.

"No argument from me," replied Cassie. "We'd be nuts to stay here any longer."

The *Evening Headlines* fanfare began to play on the television set. Cassie pulled up the hood of her yellow slicker, took a deep breath, and stepped out onto the balcony.

Through the open door, she watched Eliza Blake welcome the audience and lead directly to the report from Sarasota.

Images of lines of fleeing traffic and people camped out at the evacuation center filled the screen, along with the predictable shots of roaring waves and jiggling palm trees. The pictures Felix had taken at the marina and from Harry Lewis's boat rounded out the piece, along with a sound bite from Jerry Dean about potential economic hardships and a spokesman from the National Hurricane Center comparing Giselle with past storms.

"Ten seconds," warned the voice from the New York control room through Cassie's earpiece.

She had memorized her final scripted line. Cassie looked into Felix's camera lens as she heard her recorded voice say, "Sarasotans are hoping that Giselle will have mercy on them but, realistically, they are, at the same time, preparing for the worst."

"Cue, Cassie," came the voice in the earpiece just as a wind gust swept through the balcony, blowing Cassie into the iron safety railing. Wincing with pain, she struggled to regain her balance.

"Eliza, as you can see, the winds are getting stronger," Cassie shouted through the roar of the wind, "and forecasters have issued their hurricane warning. They are now predicting that Giselle will crash into this area overnight. Eliza?" She tossed back to the studio.

"Cassie Sheridan, on hurricane watch in Sarasota, Florida," said Eliza Blake, safe and dry in New York.

Cassie pulled out the earpiece and ran back into the hotel room. She grabbed the towel Felix held out, wiped her soaked face, and vowed that this was the last time she would cover one of these natural disaster nightmares. Someone else could have the pleasure, she thought as she rubbed her throbbing arm.

CHAPTER
74

The police car rolled into the emergency room bay at Sarasota Memorial Hospital. The officer helped the boy from the backseat and led him inside.

"He's out of it," Sheriff's Deputy Savadel called to the receiving nurse. "I found him on the beach on my last patrol. It looks like he might have hit his head on the pier. I don't know how long he was out there."

The nurse looked at the red and already purpling lump on the child's forehead and felt his neck for a pulse. "What was this kid doing out in a hurricane?"

"Beats me," Savadel answered in disgust. "Who knows why kids do what they do?"

"Well, he's lucky you found him." She wiped the wet, sandy hair from the boy's brow and thought of the reports she had heard of the child missing from Siesta Key.

"This couldn't be the kid that everyone's been looking for, could it?"

"No, that kid's five. This kid is much older."

The radio attached to Savadel's belt announced the next emergency.

The nurse nodded. "Go ahead. We'll take over from here."

"I'll try to check in later and see how he's doing," replied Savadel as he headed back into the storm.

Behind the partially drawn curtains, Vincent lay on a wheeled hospital bed, oblivious to the activity in the rest of the busy emergency room. His jacket lay on the bedside table where the nurse had placed it. *This kid's parents must be frantic,* she thought.

While waiting for the overstretched doctor, the nurse looked for some sort of identification, starting her search at the top.

In the breast pocket of the boy's T-shirt she found a slip of paper with a phone number on it.

CHAPTER
75

"Mom?"

"Hannah?" The last thing Cassie had been expecting was a call from her daughter.

"Are you all right, Mom?"

"Yes, I'm fine, honey."

"I just saw you on TV. It looked like you hurt yourself."

"Oh, that. That was nothing," Cassie lied. The arm ached. "I'm so glad you called, though, Hannah. I've been thinking of you, sweetheart, and wondering how you are."

"It's boring up here."

"I could take a little boring right now. Boring sounds good."

Static crackled on the cell phone line.

"Hannah?"

"Yeah?"

"I better go now. I'll call—" The phone went dead.

She'd call back later, when they got to the evacuation center. She liked thinking that Hannah had made it a point to watch her on television and that she still cared enough to be concerned when she thought her mother had hurt herself. That was something at least.

She was about to leave the hotel room when the cell phone rang again. Cassie answered, fully expecting to hear her daughter's voice calling back.

"Hannah?"

"This is Erin Duby, an ER nurse at Sarasota Memorial Hospital. To whom am I speaking?"

"This is Cassie Sheridan."

"Do you have a son?"

"No. Why do you ask?"

"We have a young boy here who had your phone number in his pocket."

"What do you mean you'll meet us at the evacuation center?" Lou-Anne screeched into the telephone. "In case you've forgotten, Webb, you have two kids. Why aren't you here where you belong? If I have to answer one more of their questions about this hurricane, I am going to go out of my mind. And now you tell me to pack them up and get to the evacuation center myself? You've got some nerve, buster."

"The world doesn't revolve around you, Lou-Anne. I have a business to run—a business, I might add, that pays for the cushy life you enjoy—and I spent the day securing it. So quit complaining and get in the car and start driving. We don't have time for your tantrums."

Her husband gave her no time to fire another salvo. Lou-Anne heard the decisive click on the line.

CHAPTER
77

Cassie gave the nurse Wendy Bayler's telephone number and jotted down directions to the hospital. Then she called Leroy's room. "You're moving the satellite truck, aren't you?"

"Of course. It's not safe to leave it here. Besides, we'll need it to transmit from the evacuation center in the morning."

"Right. Well, you and Felix go on in the truck. I'll take the Jeep and meet you there."

"Any reason?" Leroy asked.

"Nothing I care to share right now. I'll be on my beeper if you need me."

The drive to the hospital was excruciatingly slow. Cassie listened on the radio to reports of flooded roads and downed power lines.

"This is no joke, folks. You shouldn't be out

there if you don't absolutely have to be. And make sure you keep your kids inside. The sheriff's department found a boy on Siesta Beach at the Old Pier. What he was doing out there, nobody knows, but he had to be taken to the hospital."

CHAPTER
78

With Mark beside him, he had driven down the Tamiami Trail to see if he could get onto Siesta Key by way of the Stickney Point bridge, but that was closed as well. He'd pulled over when he spotted phone booths, calling the Baylers' house, hanging up when the mother answered. The kid was the one he needed to reach.

In desperation, he was driving home; there he would try to figure out what to do next. He heard the words coming from the car radio and knew where he had to go.

*   *   *

"Please don't leave me here. You said we were going to Vincent. You promised. I want to go home. I want my mommy." Mark's chest heaved as he sobbed and coughed.

"Here, take your medicine."

He felt sorry for the kid, but it couldn't be helped. He had to go to the hospital alone.

He hoped those hurricane shades on the windows would do their jobs. He hoped they would be enough.

CHAPTER
79

"What were you doing out there, anyway?"

Pale and solemn, Vincent sat on the hospital bed. His head hurt. He cast a look at the hovering nurse, refusing to answer Cassie's question.

"We reached his mother," said the nurse. "She's unable to come to get him. Normally, we might keep him for observation, but he seems all right now, and we are only keeping critical patients. His mother gave her permission for him to go to the evacuation center with you."

Cassie was concerned about the responsibility. A kid who'd hit his head should be watched, and she still had her job to do. "I'd like to call Vincent's mother."

She tried repeatedly, on her cell and on the hospital phone, but she couldn't get through. The lines must have been out.

Angry rain beat on the Jeep's metal roof. As Vincent buckled his seat belt, Cassie insisted that he explain what was going on. "We're not going anywhere until you tell me."

Realizing, finally, that this was too much for him to handle on his own, he related his story, haltingly at first. Then it poured from him, a relief. The ring on the beach that Gideon had tried to sell, how he had hidden in the bathroom while his friend was attacked, the phone call from the man who had taken his brother demanding the ring as ransom, leaving Mark's medicine and pounder at the tennis courts, the swap that never happened at the Old Pier.

"You should have told your mother, Vincent. You should have told the police."

"He said if I told the police, I wouldn't get Mark back." Vincent pleaded his justification. "I had to get him back. Everything was all my fault."

Cassie calculated the anguish the boy had been through, and she had to hold herself back from wrapping her arms around him. "It wasn't your fault, Vincent. You weren't responsible for a very bad man taking Mark. He did that."

"But I should have been there. If I was home, watching Mark like I was s'posed to, none of this would have happened."

"We can't change what's already happened, honey. All we can do is figure out what to do from here. Give me the ring, Vincent. Let me hold on to it."

He opened his jacket, zipped open the pocket, and dug inside. He handed her the ring, glad to be rid of it. Cassie slid it on her finger.

Next she pulled out her cell phone but couldn't get a connection. Cassie turned the key in the ignition and put the Jeep into drive. She'd try to reach the police again when they got to the evacuation center.

CHAPTER
80

"I'm looking for Vincent Bayler." The worried-looking man stood at the emergency room admitting desk.

"Are you his father?"

Why not?

"Yes. Where is he? I want to see him."

"I'm sorry, Mr. Bayler, but he just left." The nurse was puzzled. "Your wife said no one could come to get him. She gave permission for him to leave with someone else."

"Who? Who did he go with?"

The nurse mistook the urgency in the man's voice for understandable parental concern. She checked her clipboard. "A Cassie Sheridan. She was taking him to the evacuation center at Sarasota High School."

CHAPTER
81

Etta and Charles were glad that they had staked out their place in the high school media center. If you had to be stuck somewhere riding out a hurricane, what better spot to be than surrounded by thousands of volumes of books and recordings?

Charles contented himself with a stack of architecture books he'd pulled from the shelves. Etta, fearful of straining her eyes, helped herself to a headset and some classical music tapes.

Closing the cover of his book, Charles leaned over and pulled an earphone from his wife's ear. "Want to try again? The line might be shorter now."

"That's a good idea, dear."

The retirees made their way to the cafeteria, where soup, fruit, donuts, and coffee were being served by volunteers.

They sat together sipping their soup, each trying not to let the other know how worried they were. Charles peeled an orange and held it out to his wife. "Etta?"

She was squinting at something at the side of the cafeteria. "Charles, I think that's the boy from the beach. You know, the one I told you about? The one that found the hand the other morning."

He looked in the direction of her gaze. The boy seemed to be sitting by himself.

"You don't think he could be alone here, do you, Charles?"

"No. I'm sure he must have someone with him."

Etta continued to watch. "I'm going over to him."

"Now, Etta, don't go overreacting. I'm sure the kid's fine. You don't have to get involved."

She ignored her husband's instruction. "If it were our child, I'd want someone to check on him."

As Etta reached the boy's table, another woman approached, carrying a tray, which she set before the child. Etta smiled and explained. "I was worried when I saw him sitting all by himself." She looked at the boy. "I recognize you from Siesta Beach. I've seen you out there with your metal detector." She deliberately didn't bring up the unpleasantness with the hand.

"I've seen you around, too," said Vincent.

Cassie introduced herself.

"I'm Etta Chambers. You're his mother?"

"No, actually, I'm not. Just a friend. His mother couldn't be here."

What kind of mother wasn't with her child during a hurricane? wondered Etta, automatically wanting to take care of this boy.

"I see."

Cassie studied the older woman, well groomed and dressed in a good-quality nylon running suit. She looked like a hip grandma.

"Cassie, my head hurts." The boy rubbed his temples.

"That's to be expected, Vincent." She glanced at her watch. "I guess it wouldn't hurt to take some more Tylenol."

"What happened to him?" Etta asked with concern.

"He hit his head earlier, and he really should be watched. My problem is that I'm a reporter and I'm also here working."

"I could stay with him, if you want."

It was a tempting offer. What were the

chances that this elderly lady was a kidnap-per? Pretty darn remote. And what choice did Cassie have? She could drag Vincent along with her as she did interviews around the evacuation center, but he really should be resting. Cassie's gut told her Etta Cham-bers was safe, a straight shooter. She had to go with that feeling.

Cassie looked down at Vincent. "How does that sound?"

"I guess it would be okay." The boy shrugged.

"Good," said Etta. "My husband and I are staying in the media center. After Vincent fin-ishes eating, that's where we'll be."

CHAPTER
82

Cassie found Leroy and Felix in the crowded gymnasium.

"There you are. Finally. I can't get through to New York," declared Leroy. "The damned cell phones aren't working. We should just go on shooting and hope that we can get through later."

Cassie wasn't surprised. She hadn't been able to reach the police either.

Vincent was safe, but little Mark Bayler was out there somewhere, being held by a desperate killer. A man so crazed that he would slay an old man and kidnap a child to get back the ring that had been on Merilee Quiñones's finger.

Cassie looked at the ring that now encircled her finger. She slipped it off and held it up to catch the light from the glaring overhead gymnasium lights. There was no inscription, only the jeweler's mark. She squinted to see it better.

A flowery, scripted LS.

Leslie Sebastien. The jeweler slashed at Ringling two nights ago.

On the theory that three heads were better than one, she decided to share what she knew with Leroy and Felix.

"I saw a sheriff's car out in front when we pulled in," offered Felix after hearing her story.

"Well it's not there now," observed Cassie. "I checked with the school office. They had to go off and answer an emergency call."

CHAPTER
83

He'd heard that the new high school could hold close to two thousand evacuees. He went from classroom to classroom looking for Vincent and Cassie. Needles in a haystack. Through the busy hallways, stepping over blankets and sleeping bags, picking his way around the children passing the time by playing cards and board games on the floor. He searched each young face.

Children filled the music room, banging on the piano, beating the drums. Babies cried and mothers shushed and fathers paced.

"I haven't seen you in quite a while."

He turned to face the voice but had to look down to see where it had come from.

"Anthony. How ya doin'?" *Stay calm. Don't give yourself away.*

The little man waved his arms. "This sure is something, huh?"

"Sure is."

"Where are you camped out?"

He thought fast. "The gym. I was just stretching my legs."

Anthony nodded. "Don't forget, you promised you'd sub for me next week at the hospital. Who knows if this storm will have any little casualties, but whoever's in the pediatric unit will definitely need some cheering up."

"I'll call you about it," he said, edging away. "I'll call you."

CHAPTER
84

She was in no mood for that jerk. Gloria steered clear of Van when she saw him taking a drink from the water fountain.

She found her corner to huddle in at the end of the jammed hallway. She spread out her blanket and arranged her picnic hamper and the pile of movie and fashion magazines she had brought to pass the time.

She slathered some moisturizer over her face and hands and took a long swallow from her water bottle. Might as well make these hours count, use the time as an opportunity for a little spa treatment. She hadn't been satisfied with the way she'd looked in the rushes of yesterday's shoot that Webb had shown her. Her skin looked too dry, her hair brittle and frayed.

With her back against the wall, she stretched out to catch up on what her favorite models were sporting. Lots of leg, tight abs, and sheer blouses opened to reveal perky breasts. Gloria tightened her stomach, sucked in her breath, and lifted her legs a few inches above the blanket, holding them as long as she could.

She was letting out her breath when she saw the man standing farther down the hall, seeming to search the congestion, his face intense and glowering.

Gloria buried her head in her magazine.

She didn't want him to spot her. She didn't want him to see her without her makeup on. Nor was she in any mood to talk to him about Merilee.

When this hurricane was over, maybe she should go to the police with her suspicions.

CHAPTER
85

What great luck! There was Cassie Sheridan.

"I'll be right back," he said to his camerawoman.

With his bag slung over his shoulder, the SNN reporter picked his way across the people-scattered gym floor. When he reached Cassie, he stood aside and waited while she finished the interview she was doing.

"Cassie? Hi." He could tell she didn't recognize him right away. "Tony Whitcomb. From SNN?" he coaxed, crestfallen.

"Oh, yes, Tony. Of course."

"I have the tape I was telling you about. I didn't have a chance to mail it yet. But this is better. I can give it directly to you."

Tony's audition tape was the last thing on her mind right now, but Cassie accepted the cassette he held out to her.

"I put some of my best stuff on it. Sweeps pieces. The station spends some money then and I get to go out of town. I thought the network would like to see me in some different locations."

"Fine, Tony. I'll pass it on." She tucked the tape in her bag. She wanted to finish her interviews so she could go check on Vincent.

CHAPTER
86

It was times like this that Harrison Lewis hated being a doctor and the notoriety it could provide. People were always recognizing him, coming up to him and chatting. As if he cared.

Even in the sea of people at the evacuation center, there was no anonymity. Some old coot that he had operated on had spotted him. He stood before Harry now, raving about the changes in his life since he'd had his cataracts removed. "I can't thank you enough, Doc. The past year has been wonderful. Kitty and I can go out to dinner and go dancing at night. I don't have to worry anymore about driving in the dark."

"Glad to hear it." He wanted to get away, but he was trapped.

CHAPTER
87

As Jerry waited in line for coffee and donuts, he saw the guy who'd rented Webb's boat last week standing in the cafeteria doorway. He wanted to give the pig a piece of his mind. Leaving powder all over the head of the boat like that and raising Webb's suspicions.

But Jerry was hungry, and he didn't want to give up his place in the line. He'd get the slob later.

CHAPTER
88

"Charles, go with him," Etta urged.

"I can go by myself," Vincent insisted. She was treating him like a baby.

"Oh, Etta, stop worrying. He'll be all right. Go ahead, son. But come right back," said Charles, pointing the way to the men's room.

Etta watched as the boy walked out of the media center. Maybe Charles was right. She knew she had a tendency to be overprotective. But things happened.

He spotted the boy as he was entering the men's room and followed him inside. There were too many others using the urinals and stalls, so he went back out into the hall to wait.

The heavy door opened again and again until the sun-brightened brown hair he was looking for emerged. He grabbed Vincent's arm. "Don't say a word. If you want to see your brother again, don't say a word."

Vincent looked up with surprise at the face. "I know you," he exclaimed, disobeying the order.

He had been afraid that it might come to this. The kid could identify him. Well, he would just have to get rid of Vincent, too.

CHAPTER
90

Mark got up from the studio couch and turned off the television. It was making him scared. All those people talking about the hurricane that was hitting his town. The TV said everyone should be "vacuated" from Siesta Key.

He didn't know what "vacuated" meant, but Mark did know that Siesta Key was where his house was. The house he lived in with Vincent and Mommy.

Why didn't Mommy come and get him? Had something happened to her? Was that why she hadn't come?

He tried hard not to start crying again. That would only make his coughing worse. But the powerful wind rattling the metal shades on the windows scared him more. The sobs began, and then the coughs.

He needed a treatment.

Maybe he could give it to himself. If he propped the pounder against the wall next to the couch, maybe he could lie against it.

Mark went to the closet where he had seen the man put the pounder. Jackets and shirts hung on the closet rod. He could see the edge of the pounder sticking out from the shelf on top. Mark stretched, but he couldn't reach.

He saw the umbrella on the closet floor and picked it up. As he pointed it up at the shelf, his finger hit the button on the shaft, opening the umbrella. It popped from his grasp and nearly sent him flying backward.

As Mark went to pick the umbrella back up, he recognized the letters printed on the nylon. S-N-N.

Just like on the news.

CHAPTER
91

Row upon row of bookcases filled the media center. Cassie walked slowly along one side of the large room, looking down each aisle for Vincent. Eventually she found Etta, who introduced her to Charles Chambers.

"A pleasure to meet you," said Charles, shaking her hand. "I've seen you on television. You do nice work."

"Thank you," acknowledged Cassie, glancing around the room. "Where's Vincent?"

"He went to the bathroom," said Etta. "He should be right back."

"How's his headache?"

"He hasn't been complaining."

"Good," said Cassie.

Etta looked anxiously toward the door. "Maybe you should go check on him, Charles."

Her husband looked at her with resigned exasperation but got up anyway. *How nice it must be,* thought Cassie, speculating that these two had spent a devoted lifetime together.

Vincent's headache might be gone, but hers was beginning to throb. She hadn't eaten since lunch. She opened her bag to search for her bottle of Tylenol. At the top of the mess inside was Tony Whitcomb's audition tape. On the typewritten label the words MARDI GRAS caught her eye. For Cassie, Mardi Gras would be forever connected with Maggie Lynch.

She took out the cassette and studied the listing on it.

- South Florida's only Thanksgiving Day Parade, Miami
- Mardi Gras, New Orleans
- The Kentucky Derby, Louisville

Sweeps stories, Tony had bragged. Cassie's mind raced. The predominant sweeps periods were November, February, and May.

Sweeps months. The months when television pulled out all the stops to get ratings. The months that decided advertising rates.

The same months when the clown rapist had struck, attacking his victims in each of the cities featured on Tony Whitcomb's audition tape.

Cassie's synapses continued firing. Whitcomb was the reporter who had interviewed Vincent on the beach the morning the boy found Merilee's hand. He had also been at Ringling the night Leslie Sebastien was murdered.

The ruby glistened from the ring on Cassie's finger, a ring most likely crafted by Leslie Sebastien. The ring Gideon had been killed for. The ring the kidnapper was demanding as ransom for Mark Bayler.

All coincidence? Maybe. Still, Cassie didn't like the feeling she had.

"Etta, I'm sorry. I have to go," Cassie said, as she hurried to gather up her things. "Tell Vincent I'll be back as soon as I can."

CHAPTER
92

He took the boy to a place where it felt somehow safe. In his search, he had come upon the regular, not-so-little theater with a stage and drapes and rows of seats where students and parents could watch school productions. Plays meant makeup.

He'd gone backstage and poked around. Sets and props and costumes hung on racks. And makeup. Cases of makeup.

He'd found a small room at the back of the stage, a room where Vincent sat with him now. An empty, isolated room, a room with an exit to the parking lot. It was tailor-made.

"The ring. Give it to me."

"I don't have it."

"Don't be cute with me. Your brother's life depends on it, Vincent. Hand the ring over."

"I'm telling you, I don't have it."

"Well, where is it?"

The tone of the man's voice shook Vincent, and he wasn't sure what to do. He didn't want to tell that he had given the ring to Cassie, but he had to get Mark back.

"I'm at the end of my patience, Vincent. And your little brother is all by himself in this storm. If I get the ring, he goes free. It's in your hands. Now, damn it, where's that ring?"

CHAPTER
93

"I can't find him."

"What do you mean, you can't find him?"

"Just what I said, Etta. Vincent's not in the bathroom."

Ettta started for the media center door, but Charles held her back. "I'll go look for him," he instructed. "You wait here in case he comes back."

Charles struggled through the hallway, calling the boy's name, paying no attention to the startled expressions of the people camped out there.

"Vincent. . . . Vincent."

"What does he look like, mister?"

"Eleven years old, brown hair, brown eyes, wearing a navy T-shirt."

"I saw a boy like that," someone volunteered, gesturing down the hallway. "He was walking with a man in that direction."

CHAPTER
94

Cassie was out of breath, her heart pounding. Leroy and Felix weren't in the gym or any of the half dozen classrooms she'd checked. Her search could go on forever, while Tony Whitcomb was right here in this building.

Don't panic. Think. Think.

"Attention, please. Will any doctors or nurses in the house please report to the main office? Doctors and nurses, to the main office, please."

The public address system. She could page Leroy.

CHAPTER
95

He stuffed a sock in Vincent's mouth and tied him to the chair with the belts he'd stripped from the hanging costumes, pulling the bonds nice and tight. "There, that should hold you," he muttered. "Now don't go getting any ideas about trying to get loose. Not if you want to see your brother again."

He left the boy in the room and walked out to the stage. At the side he parted the curtain, ever so slightly, peeking out at the auditorium. The people who sat there just dozed or talked among themselves, not noticing him.

How was he going to get Cassie Sheridan to come to him?

CHAPTER
96

Cassie waited outside the office door for Leroy and Felix to respond to the page. Minutes passed. After what seemed like an eternity, she saw them approaching. "Thank God, you're here," she declared, launching into her explanation of what she suspected.

"Tony Whitcomb?" asked Felix with skepticism. "The local news reporter?"

Leroy's face contorted. "The guy who wants to come work at the network? He didn't look like a rapist or murderer to me."

"And exactly what does a murderer look like, Leroy?" Cassie couldn't keep the sarcasm from her voice. "I'm telling you, Tony Whitcomb could be guilty of the rape of Maggie Lynch and those other young women— and maybe a kidnapping and a couple of murders as well."

CHAPTER
97

He came down from the stage and walked to the back of the auditorium, where a phone hung from the wall. He picked up the receiver and listened.

"Yes? May I help you?"

"Who is this?"

"This is the office. May I help you?"

"I'm trying to reach someone. Is it possible to page her?"

"You can leave a message, and I will call the person to come and get it."

"Thank you. Would you please ask Cassie Sheridan to meet Vincent in the auditorium?"

"Oh, Ms. Sheridan was just here. Let me see if I can catch her. Otherwise, I'll page her and see that she gets your message."

"Thank you. Thank you very much."

As he hung up the phone, he felt a tap on his shoulder. It was Tony Whitcomb.

"Hey, what are you doing here? I thought you were sick," accused the reporter.

"I *am* sick, but I don't want to *die,*" Brian answered, trying to appear nonchalant. "I wasn't going to sit in my condo and wait this thing out." He changed the subject. "Who are you shooting with?"

"That new girl, Carla."

"How is she?"

"Not bad." Tony turned around and looked for his camerawoman. "I gotta go, Brian. Some of us have to work."

Brian watched with relief as Tony walked away.

CHAPTER
98

By the glum expression on her husband's face, Etta could tell that he hadn't found Vincent. "Oh, Charles, what are we going to do? I promised to take care of that child."

He thought he may have just wasted precious time searching the halls and neighboring classrooms, but Charles hadn't wanted to return to his wife without their charge safely in tow. "Etta, I'm afraid the boy didn't just wander off."

"What do you mean?"

"Somebody said they saw a boy fitting Vincent's description walking away with a man."

CHAPTER
99

Cassie stayed in the front lobby, anxiously shifting her weight from one foot to the other. Leroy and Felix had posted themselves at other school entrances, all of them waiting for a police car to show up.

"Cassie Sheridan. Please come to the office. Cassie Sheridan, to the office, please."

She wasn't going to answer now, not when, finally, she could see a sheriff's department vehicle had pulled up outside. A woman with a baby in her arms alighted from the backseat. Cassie held the lobby door open for them, yelling out to the officer.

"I've got another call to respond to, ma'am."

Cassie ran into the rain, leaning into the open window. "This is an emergency. I'm Cassie Sheridan with KEY News. Please, I promise you, this is an emergency."

"Get in."

Cassie handed Tony Whitcomb's tape to the deputy. He listened to her story and radioed for backup. Then he left his car at the curb and followed her inside.

CHAPTER
100

He had enough material to do several pieces. Now he had to hope that the microwave truck parked in front of the school would be able to transmit back to the station.

Tony was making his way to the entrance, composing his script in his mind as he went, when he heard the excited voice.

"There he is. There's Tony Whitcomb."

At first he smiled, thinking someone in the lobby had recognized him as a celebrity. Then his expression turned to one of puzzlement as he saw that it was Cassie Sheridan who was pointing at him. Finally he frowned as the sheriff's deputy took his arm.

CHAPTER
101

Finally, there might be some closure for Maggie Lynch's family and for the other rape victims, Cassie thought as she watched Tony walking off with his police escort. Closure for them and justice for Merilee Quiñones.

And Cassie couldn't help but hope that if Tony Whitcomb did indeed turn out to be the clown rapist, she had solved the FBI's case and, perhaps, Pamela Lynch would drop the lawsuit that had wrecked Cassie's life. But most important was justice for the women who had been brutalized by this monster.

"Cassie Sheridan. Please come to the office." The noise from the loudspeaker intruded. The page. She had to answer that page.

Charles Chambers, his mouth set in a grim line, was standing at the office desk.

"What's wrong?"

"I'm sorry to have to say this, but Vincent's gone."

"What do you mean, gone?"

"He didn't come back from the bathroom, and we can't find him."

The woman behind the desk listened, wanting to be of some help. "Excuse me, Ms. Sheridan?" she interrupted. "You have a message from a Vincent here." She handed a slip of paper to Cassie.

Cassie read the note with relief. "Don't worry, Mr. Chambers. Vincent is all right. He wants me to meet him in the auditorium."

"Down to the end of the hall and to the right." The woman pointed as Cassie sped out the door, leaving Charles without a chance to mention the man who had been seen with the boy.

CHAPTER
102

Idle hands are the devil's workshop. Or was it idle minds? What was it that his mother used to say in her endless rants? No matter. In this case, hands worked well enough for him.

While he waited for Cassie, he kept his hands busy. Drawing, painting, powdering. The makeup kits were missing some of the supplies he preferred, but Brian made do, his tension easing as he watched his face transform in the case mirror.

He wished he had worn the blue contact lenses this time, but he hadn't known he was going to be meeting up with her. He had a feeling that Cassie might have a hankering for blue-eyed men, and he wanted to make things as pleasurable as possible for her.

At first.

After he'd had his way with her, though,

Cassie wasn't going to experience any more pleasure.

The boy's eyes were trained on him, wide and brown.

"Don't worry, Vincent. Cassie's coming."

CHAPTER
103

Where was Vincent and why did he come here? Cassie walked down the gentle slope of the auditorium floor, searching for the familiar face. Was he playing some sort of game?

This isn't the time to be fooling around, Vincent, she thought. When she found him, she was going to tell him so in no uncertain terms. Right after she let him know that the police had the man who had kidnapped Mark.

Okay, Vincent. I can play the game. Cassie climbed the steps at the side of the stage and slid behind the curtain.

CHAPTER
104

The assistant principal's office was empty, save for the sheriff's deputy and Tony Whitcomb.

"You have the right to remain silent. Anything you say can and will be used against you in a court of law."

"You're out of your mind. Do you know who I am? You have no right to hold me here."

"Sorry, Mr. Whitcomb, but as soon as the storm lets up, I'm going to take you in for questioning."

"About what?"

He knew he probably shouldn't, but he couldn't resist. The deputy tossed the tape on the desk. "This. But before we get to your traveling escapades, you better tell me where Mark Bayler is."

CHAPTER
105

Except for the props and scenery flats, the backstage was empty. "Vincent? Vincent, are you here?" In the dimness, Cassie listened, hearing the creak of an opening door.

"Vincent? Come on now. This isn't funny," she called, starting in the direction of the noise. The floorboards squeaked beneath her feet.

"I think we're going to find Mark now," she called, trying to entice him. "I'm not kidding, Vincent. Come out."

Light streamed from the crack in the door at the back of the stage. Cassie pushed against the wood.

Bound and gagged, the boy sat in the chair.

"Vincent!" She rushed to him.

His frightened eyes looked behind her.

CHAPTER
106

This wasn't getting him anywhere. He had work to do. Leroy was tired of waiting around for police who might never show up to tell them about Cassie's, as far as he was concerned, far-fetched notion. Cassie might be losing it, Leroy speculated.

He had talked to a friend at the Broadcast Center who told him Valeria Delaney was getting the Justice beat. Cassie had been preoccupied for the rest of the afternoon after that phone call—a phone call Leroy suspected had delivered the news that she was officially out of the Washington mix, never to return. This whole scenario she had cooked up about Tony Whitcomb being the clown rapist could just be the result of Cassie's desperate wish to redeem herself.

He left his post and headed back to the front lobby, stopping along the way to get Felix. "This is ridiculous, Felix. Let's go. We're wasting our time."

CHAPTER
107

"Not in front of the boy. Please, not in front of Vincent," Cassie pleaded, the cold, steel blade against her neck. "Please, let him go."

"Sorry, Cassie, but I can't. He's seen too much. Now, go ahead. Take off your clothes."

She tried to focus, struggling to remember her conversation with Will Clayton. Had that been only three days ago? It seemed like another lifetime. She had to pull the FBI agent's observations from her memory bank. Her life and Vincent's depended on it.

A compensatory rapist, Will had said. An inadequate personality, the rape assuaging his self-doubts. A core fantasy was that the victim will enjoy the rape and fall in love with him.

"Please, I can't relax with the boy here."

The bloodshot brown eyes peering from the grotesque face studied her, considering her words. She was older than the others he had chosen but was in fine shape just the same. If Cassie was calm, it would be much more satisfying for him. And he wanted to enjoy this before he had to kill her.

"I can't let Vincent go, Cassie. But I'll move him out of the room so we can have our privacy."

CHAPTER
108

"The city of Sarasota is in for one helluva lawsuit," Tony threatened. "The thought that I went around raping people is absolutely preposterous. And as for kidnapping the Bayler boy, how dare you accuse me of that? I'm going sue the ass off this town."

The deputy was starting to think that Tony's protestations might be based on truth.

"Go ahead, check with SNN," Tony urged. "They can tell you. I was at the station all yesterday afternoon and evening. I couldn't have kidnapped Mark Bayler."

CHAPTER
109

"What do you like? What turns you on, Cassie?"

The floor felt cold against her bare back. Her legs were crossed and rigid. She held her folded arms against her breasts, covering herself.

His powdered face brushed against hers. "Relax, Cassie," he whispered. "It won't hurt. Relax."

CHAPTER
110

The knotted belts cut into his flesh.

Outside the door, Vincent struggled in his chair, twisting his wrists against the bonds. If he could just loosen the belts enough to slip his hand through, he'd be able to pull the gag from his mouth and call out.

Help was just on the other side of the curtain.

CHAPTER
111

The electric ceiling light dimmed with a momentary loss of power and then brightened again, its glare beating down on her.

The hurricane. She had forgotten about it. The sound of the wind roared through the walls.

"I'm sorry, but I can't relax. I want to, but I can't."

The steel point pressed at her neck. "It's up to you, Cassie. You can make it easier on yourself."

"Maybe if we talked a little first. I'm worried about Mark. If I knew that Mark was all right, I think that would help."

"The kid's fine. I left him safe and dry."

"At your house?"

Brian leered beneath the makeup's frown. "I know what you're trying to do, Cassie.

Pumping me for information like all you reporters do."

It wouldn't hurt to answer her, would it?
She wasn't going to have the chance to tell
anyone. If knowing where the boy was would
loosen Cassie up, it was worth the trade.
"Yes. He's at my house. Feel better now?"

She tried not to cringe as his fevered body
pressed against her.

"You know, I admire you." She had to keep
him talking, play into his need for reassurance, buy herself time. "You've stumped the
FBI. The country's premier law enforcement
organization has been trying to find you, but
you've been too smart for them. You must be
proud of that."

That was right, he should be proud. He
wanted more of her praise.

"The FBI checked all the flights going out
of Miami, New Orleans, and Louisville on the
days when you left those women's cars at the
airports," Cassie continued. "There was no
one name that appeared on all three flights."

"That's because I just parked the cars
there and took cabs back to the hotel. Tony
didn't even know I had been gone. He was
too busy getting his beauty sleep."

"Clever. Very clever." Slowly, she raised her hand to caress his face. "And why the makeup? You don't need makeup. You're so handsome without it."

"It's a long story." The brown eyes welled up.

"We have time."

"No, Cassie, we don't. Time's up."

CHAPTER
112

"I'm Leroy Barry, with KEY News. Could you page Cassie Sheridan for me, please?"

The woman at the desk sighed. What was she, Cassie Sheridan's personal messenger service?

A gray-haired man who'd been waiting at the side of the office approached Leroy. "Excuse me. I heard you mention Cassie Sheridan. Do you know if she found that boy? My wife and I are very worried."

Leroy listened to Charles Chambers's story.

CHAPTER
113

Faintly, Cassie heard her name being called from the auditorium's loudspeakers. She couldn't be sure if the man on top of her heard it, too.

They were looking for her. Please, let them find her. She just needed some more time.

"Thank you for talking to me. I'm feeling better," she lied. "Just one last thing, I promise."

Beads of perspiration dotted the chalky forehead. "One more, that's it."

"Merilee Quiñones, the woman whose hand was found on the beach. Tell me about her." Cassie deliberately left her question open-ended.

Brian pulled back, reached down, and took Cassie's hand. Holding it up, he gazed at the ruby ring.

"This was Merilee's," he said, his tone low. "This was supposed to symbolize the life we would have together. I had such hopes."

For just an instant Cassie almost felt sorry for this pathetic creature pinning her to the floor.

"But Merilee turned out to be just like my mother," he said, turning the ring on Cassie's finger. "She mocked me. She ruined everything by mocking me. We struggled, she fell overboard. She wasn't supposed to die."

But she did, you crazed lunatic, thought Cassie. *She did die. You ended Merilee's life and Leslie Sebastien's and the old fisherman's. You devastated the lives of those young women you attacked, and your actions led to an emotional trauma so severe that Maggie Lynch ended up taking hers.*

Yes, Cassie had probably provided the final straw by going public with the young woman's agony, and for that she would be forever haunted. *But you, you tortured, sick soul, are responsible for Maggie's death. As responsible as if you pushed her from the Watergate terrace yourself.*

"Yes, Merilee was supposed to wear this

ring in the life I wanted us to have, but I'm glad you're wearing it now, Cassie."

Cassie turned her head, wretching violently, as the overhead light suddenly went out.

CHAPTER
114

The dim light went out, leaving the backstage area in total darkness. Vincent heard voices rising in protest from the other side of the curtain.

His face contorted in pain as he twisted his wrists against the belt. He could feel it loosening.

One more time, twisting with all his might, freed him. He wanted to run to Cassie and help her, but he didn't like the odds. The man was strong, and he had that knife. Vincent knew he probably wouldn't be able to overpower him.

Trust your instincts, Cassie had said.

He had to get help.

In the darkness, Vincent felt his way to the curtain, one hand stretched out in front of him, pulling the gag from his mouth with the other.

CHAPTER
115

As Cassie vomited, by instinct, he dropped her hand and pulled away. By instinct, but it was a mistake.

In the pitch darkness, Cassie groped for the knife. There was the blade. Cold, smooth.

Steady, steady. Her fingers caressed the deadly steel, searching for the texture of the handle.

He was looking for it, too. "Don't try anything foolish, Cassie." His hiss pierced the blackness.

"I won't," Cassie promised breathlessly.

That wasn't a lie, she thought as her hand gripped the knife handle. This wasn't foolish. It was smart.

Distract him. You've got to distract him.

"I'm ready for you now." She did lie this time. "Where are you?"

"I'm here, Cassie. I'm here."

"Come to me." She forced out the words, praying she wouldn't get sick again. She felt the heat of his body as he laid himself on top of her. The rancid smell of his perspiration made her gag.

"What's wrong?" he asked.

"Nothing. Nothing's wrong," she lied again. Her eyes stared into the blackness as the clown's greasy mouth searched for hers. As she tasted the waxy paint, her hand tightened around the knife.

Now. Now.

With all her strength, she thrust into the darkness, hearing the dull puncturing sound.

When the lights flickered on again, Cassie saw how well she had hit her mark.

Smeared with blood, she was crouched on the floor trying to cover herself when they arrived.

Leroy scanned the room, holding out his

arm to block Vincent's entrance. "Wait back there, kid," he instructed with firmness.

Leroy took off his jacket, averting his eyes as he handed it to Cassie.

"Who'd a thunk I'd ever be glad to see you?" Cassie managed to joke through her tears.

EPILOGUE

Sunday, August 25

"Congratulations, Cassie, on the work you've done this past week," Yelena praised from New York. "You've been an example of the best traditions of KEY News."

"Thanks."

While another KEY News correspondent had been sent in to report on Giselle's aftermath for the last three days, Cassie had been featured on every KEY News broadcast with her stories of the clown rapist and his crimes. Even *Hourglass* had wanted a segment. Brian Mueller was recovering from his stab wound. Legal experts speculated that he would enter an insanity defense and end up spending the rest of his life in a psychiatric facility.

That Yelena was calling her from home, on a Sunday, signaled Cassie's repolished status in the news division. Her suddenly attentive agent had tracked her down as well, informing her that he had gotten calls from ABC, CBS, and NBC about the status of her contract. All three networks were interested in signing her.

Yelena wasn't dumb. Cassie was a hot property again, and Yelena knew she had to do some major league repair work on their relationship if KEY News had any chance of keeping Cassie Sheridan.

Cassie knew this, too. Right now, though, deciding which news organization her next contract would be with didn't interest her. She wanted to get home, to Hannah and Jim.

"And the best news comes from the legal department, Cassie. Pamela Lynch is considering dropping the lawsuit since you were instrumental in catching the rapist."

Cassie did not react as Yelena expected. There was no enthusiasm in her voice. Just a quiet "Thank God."

"Let's talk tomorrow, Cassie, about what your future will hold. I'll call you at the Miami Bureau in the morning."

"I won't be there, Yelena."

"Oh?"

"From here, I'm flying to Washington. I want to see my daughter." It was a statement, not a request for permission.

"Of course, of course," Yelena said hastily. "I'll call you there, then."

Whatever, thought Cassie. Her boss's call meant little to her now. The only ones that mattered were the ones from Jim and Hannah, worried about her and wanting her to come home.

Before she went to the airport, Cassie had a stop to make. "Siesta Key, please. 603 Calle de Peru."

She looked out the taxi window at the city cleanup crews clearing away Giselle's remaining debris of fallen palm fronds and soggy trash. Passing the marina, she spotted Jerry Dean's orange baseball cap, its wearer directing the righting of a capsized boat. The taxi traveled on, making several detours around still-flooded streets.

Over the North Bridge, past The Old Salty

Dog, now reopened for lunchtime business, through Siesta Village, its shopkeepers sweeping the sandy sidewalks in front of their shops. As the cab turned onto Calle de Peru, Cassie caught sight of Mark and Vincent playing in front of their house, Wendy watching her boys from the stoop.

Vincent ran up to the car as Cassie paid the driver and gave him directions on when and where to pick her up again.

"I've been waiting for you," said the boy.

"I told you I would come."

She talked a bit with Wendy, accepting the mother's thanks yet again.

"At least something good has come from all this." Wendy smiled. "Mr. and Mrs. Chambers have volunteered to watch the boys for me when I need them. They said they'd like to be surrogate grandparents."

"Hey, that's great," Cassie responded. "That should make things a little easier for you." She gave a last pat to Mark's soft, shining hair.

Cassie turned to Vincent. "You ready?"

"Yep."

Together, Cassie and Vincent walked to their destination in the village center. They sat on the wooden bench in front of Big

Olaf's, licking their double-scoop ice cream cones.

She eyed the bandages on his thin wrists. "Does it still hurt?"

"Not much." He shrugged.

Cassie doubted the boy would tell her even if the bondage cuts throbbed.

"I guess I won't see you again," said Vincent, chocolate rimming the sides of his mouth.

"I don't know about that," answered Cassie, looking around. "This looks like a great place to vacation. I'd like to come back sometime with my daughter."

"Your daughter's lucky," Vincent said softly, studying his cone.

"Hannah doesn't always think so. But I want to change that."

"She must be nuts. I wish I had a mother like you."

Cassie returned his highest compliment. "I'd be proud to have a son like you, Vincent. But, you know, your mother is a good woman, and she's doing the best she can to take care of you and Mark. She loves you very much."

"She's all right, I guess."

Cassie didn't want Vincent fantasizing

about how wonderful it would be with a mother other than his own. Wendy was the one he had. It was only her financial situation that left her so frazzled, that made their lives so tough.

She licked her ice cream, resolving to get in touch with Sarge Tucker. After the hurricane, the band promoter had announced that he was donating his proceeds from "Nobody Knows" to local charities. Maybe he was doing it from the goodness of his heart, maybe from guilt if the song was Merilee's. It didn't really matter, now that Merilee was dead. But Cassie wanted to see some of that money funneled to the Bayler family. She had a feeling she could persuade Sarge to make that happen.

The cab pulled up in front of the ice cream shop.

Cassie rose from the bench. "I have your number and you have mine. I'll call you in a few days, okay?"

"Promise?"

"Promise." She leaned down to hug the boy who, to Cassie's pleasure, hugged her in return. "You're a good, smart boy, Vincent Bayler," she whispered. "I see great things for you, and I should know. Remember? I always trust my instincts."

Cassie waved from the rear window until the child was out of sight and then turned to look straight ahead. In a few hours she would be with Jim and Hannah. It wasn't going to be easy, but she was determined to make things right between her daughter and herself. And she hadn't given up on Jim either. They had shared so much but lost their way. She wanted to try to find it again.

She had misplaced her priorities, concentrated on her work at her family's expense. She hoped they could forgive her so they could go forward together. But, no matter what happened with Jim and Hannah, no matter what her career might hold, Cassie felt an inner calm as the sunlight streamed through the cab's windows.

She had learned, the hard way, perhaps life's most important lesson: Never take your blessings for granted.